The man jumped from the Vette the instant it stopped. "Hey, you . . . dumbshit. Where'd you learn to drive?"

Carl smiled "You couldn't be talkin' to me, could you, boy?"

"Yeah, dumbshit, I'm talkin' to you." He walked from beside the Vette and toward Lee and Browne. "What's LFL stand for? Little Fat Ladies?"

Marc slid the Smith from its holster slowly, but he kept it out of sight. "Leeco Freight Lines, shitface. You want to complain, headquarters is in Dallas. Now I suggest you mount up in that hot machine of yours and beat it."

"And what if I don't," the man challenged.

"Marc's face turned stone hard. He nodded toward Carl. "Then him and me and the boys from Massachusetts are gonna rearrange your bad attitude."

"What boys from Massachusetts?"

Marc pulled out the 9mm automatic and leveled it at the man's face. "Two of my best friends . . . Smith & Wesson."

Bantam Books by Bob Ham:

Overload #1: PERSONAL WAR
Overload #2: THE WRATH
Overload #3: HIGHWAY WARRIORS
Overload #4: TENNESSEE TERROR
Overload #5: ATLANTA BURN

OVERLOAD, Book 6

NEBRASKA NIGHTMARE

Bob Ham

BANTAM BOOKS
NEW YORK · TORONTO · LONDON · SYDNEY · AUCKLAND

NEBRASKA NIGHTMARE
A Bantam Book / April 1990

ISBN 0-553-28475-4

Published simultaneously in the United States and Canada

Bantam Books are published by Bantam Books, a division of Bantam Doubleday Dell Publishing Group, Inc. Its trademark, consisting of the words "Bantam Books" and the portrayal of a rooster, is Registered in U.S. Patent and Trademark Office and in other countries. Marca Registrada. Bantam Books, 666 Fifth Avenue, New York, New York 10103.

PRINTED IN THE UNITED STATES OF AMERICA

RAD   0 9 8 7 6 5 4 3 2 1

This one's for Linda Davis, rising country music superstar, whose timeless voice and constant smile still send chills up my spine after all these years . . . for Lang Scott, her husband and a powerful vocalist in his own right, and Hillary, their beautiful daughter.

The love and friendship of your family has always been and will always remain so very special to mine. . . . May your star forever shine as brilliantly as your smile and rise higher than any of us ever dared to dream.

All the best. . . .

I'll never give up for I may have a streak of luck before I die.

—THOMAS EDISON (July 25, 1869)

———

I have accepted the challenge and I will stop at nothing to see the carnivorous ones . . . the ones who take pleasure from the pain of Innocents . . . swept away by the cleansing power of hellfire.

—MARC LEE

CHAPTER ONE

Every eye in the recreation hall was fixed on the television. Behind each pair of those eyes was a country-music fan. And this was, without question, the biggest night for country-music fans around the world. The Country Music Association's award night drew not only the peers of those chosen for honor but also fans who were lucky enough to get a ticket to see the event. Those not fortunate enough to see the happening live could be a part of it from the comfort of their living rooms by simply switching on the television.

Richie Halloway was one of the unfortunate. But unlike millions of music fans who, just like him, watched the show on television, Halloway's misfortune wasn't limited to the impersonal confinement of television. His confinement, imposed by the Nineteenth Judicial Circuit Court of Nebraska, was for ninety-nine years and a day. Practically interpreted, life in prison.

Those around Halloway in the Nebraska State Penitentiary recreation hall were no more fortunate. They too had broken the rules of society, and now they paid their debt. That debt was hard time . . . one day at a time.

The television announcer read the nominees' names for the Song of the Year Award. And the rec hall, normally buzzing with obscenities from macho voices, was smothered in the silence of a tense hush. Everyone listened, waited. The anticipation was at least equal that felt by the nominees for the coveted award, who sat decked-out in glamorous finery several hundred miles away at the Opry House in Nashville.

1

Even the prison guards, the screws, in the rec hall were captured by the silence. There were four of them, and they stood enjoying the nervous anticipation of the announcement. The guards had positioned themselves strategically along the rec-hall walls. Two of them were unusually tense; inside the joint, word traveled quickly. And the word was that Richie Halloway's song, the one prisoners and guards alike had heard him sing either in person or on tape for over two years, might well be tonight's winner. And if his creation won, a potentially volatile situation could develop almost instantly in the atmosphere of victory.

The celebrity announcer opened the secret envelope. His voice filled the television speaker. "And the winner is—Caryn Collins and . . ."

Whistles and cheers at the mention of Caryn Collins drowned out the name of the song. Men jumped up from their seats, clapping and rejoicing. Everyone in the room yelled, and for the first time since the guard had been killed eight months ago, everybody smiled.

Almost everybody.

At a table with three of his closest companions, Richie Halloway wasn't smiling. He wasn't smiling because he was deep in thought. Devoured by hate. His eyes burned red, and his lips were clenched so tightly that his cheekbones jutted out on the sides of his face. He gritted his teeth. His short brown hair almost bristled from the anger scorching his soul. Halloway looked at his friends, polling them individually with his eyes. His lips didn't move to speak, but he had his answer. The decision was unanimous.

Halloway nodded his head.

Three prison companions stood from the table and moved through the crowd. Halloway did the same thing. They dispersed, each going a separate way and mingling into the crowd of cheering prisoners.

Richie Halloway was the first to reach his intended target. A screw stood by the double doors, the only exit from the rec hall.

The guard grinned and offered his hand to Halloway. "Congratulations, Richie. Too bad you'll never have a chance to spend the money you'll make from that song. Too damned bad."

Halloway ignored the open hand. His facial expression was cold and callous, not at all like a man who had written a song that a nation thought was the best of them all. "Yeah, too damned bad about a lot of things."

Richie's right arm came around in a sweeping arc directed straight at the guard's neck. And in his hand a prison knife, fabricated from scrap metal in the machine shop, gleamed for a microinstant before blood from the guard's neck dulled its finish.

The startled guard reacted by swinging his arm up to block the attack. He was too slow and far too late. A look of fear and disbelief locked his eyes open wide as he slumped to the floor. His final attempt to scream a warning to the other guards came harmlessly from his throat as little more than a death gurgle.

Halloway grabbed the guard's keys, his portable radio, and a stun gun. He pushed the door open slowly and ran unnoticed from the rec hall into the prison yard.

On the other side of the hall, Cliff Scott threaded his way through the inmates. The long-haired, bearded convict was doing life without parole for killing a cop six years earlier. In the weeks before, when he and Halloway had planned the escape, Scott reasoned that if necessary, one more murder wouldn't really make a difference. Life in prison or death . . . it was all the same.

He reached his mark. The man was looking the other way. "Hey, screw."

The guard turned and faced Scott. "Yeah?"

"Bye!" Scott thrust a homemade knife into the guard's esophagus and twisted so hard that the guard was almost pinned to the wall.

The guard instinctively struggled to get the blade from his throat. He fought for air to soothe his burning lungs. His hands almost reached Scott's before they fell limp and dropped to his side. Blood poured from the wound and covered Scott's hands as he jerked the blade free and lowered the knife to his side. He wiped it clean on the dead man's uniform, then retrieved the guard's radio and stun gun. He smiled. "You bastard, I hope you don't have AIDS."

Scott took a quick look around the hall and moved toward the door. Inmates were still standing and cheering, most oblivious to the brazen escape attempt under way. When he was satisfied that no one was going to sound an alarm, he moved toward the double doors Richie Halloway had used seconds before. As he moved through the crowd, he could feel freedom lurking just beyond his reach. And soon that freedom would be recognized, somewhere just outside of the outer security fence. Scott knew that once he tasted sweet freedom one more time, he would never, ever come back inside the walls of hell . . . regardless of the cost. Even if it meant losing his life.

Ray Hartley, a consecutive lifer, had reached his target seconds after Scott. He had also used a prison knife to terminate a guard. Hartley was one of the most eager to escape. He had allowed the thought of two consecutive life sentences to fester like an untreated open wound. And, like a wound, it had infected his brain.

Nine years earlier, he had killed his girlfriend and her father on a remote Nebraska farm. During the course of his lovelorn vengeance, he had made one small error—his girlfriend's mother. He had left her for dead on the kitchen floor of the farmhouse, but she survived. An extremely costly mistake. The error of his negligence came back to haunt him when the prosecution's main witness was also an intended victim. But as his mental infection deepened, he vowed he would not make the same mistake twice. The next time, and there would be a next time, the puritanical old bitch wouldn't say anything to anyone. Ever. And if securing the opportunity to heal an old wound meant dying, then so be it. After all, his heart had died nine years ago on a dusty Nebraska backroad when the only person he had ever loved told him she didn't return that love.

Hartley had made himself a vow: Nothing short of death would stop him from leaving his prison.

His target was the screw at the front of the hall, opposite the rear exit doors. The guard was looking the other way when Hartley came up behind him. He tapped the guard on the shoulder with his left hand, his prison-special knife clutched tightly in his right. The guard jerked around, startled. Hartley slammed the four-inch knife into the man's groin before the guard could speak. He twisted it with all of his strength. The guard's mouth flew open in an attempt to scream, but Hartley's left forearm crashed into the man's esophagus and riveted him to the wall. The guard's windpipe collapsed, shutting off his life-giving breath.

Hartley jerked the knife free and gave it an insurance plunge into the guard's solar plexus. When he felt no more resistance, he released his pressure on the guard's neck and let the lifeless corpse collapse to the floor.

There was no turning back. Hartley retrieved the guard's accessories and turned to work his way to the doors at the opposite end of the hall. As he pivoted to move forward, four silent blank faces stared at him. He snarled and gritted his teeth, jerking the bloody knife out in front of his chest. All four inmates turned the other way and resumed clapping.

Hartley worked his way along the rec-hall wall until the double doors were in sight. He glanced back for one final look at the bowels of hell and then disappeared through the doors into the night.

Lionel Lewis half smiled when he approached the guard he was to terminate. And he, like Scott and Hartley, knew that one more murder wouldn't make a difference in the time he had to serve inside the walls of hell. He had only one life, and the court had taken that. Prison had been home to Lewis for years. He was the youngest of the escapees. At the age of twenty, he had been adjudged an habitual offender. His sentence had been life in prison without parole.

Lewis, in the fruition of his life of crime, had permitted his criminal rage to ripen at age thirteen when he killed two convenience-store clerks during a robbery. His life went downhill from there. Although he served less than a year for his first murders because of his tender age, the time behind bars hardened him. For the remaining five years, he was in and out of legal trouble. The final straw came when he raped a ten-year-old girl in southern

Nebraska. The jury, he knew, had no mercy for a crazy nineteen-year-old nigger who'd raped a white girl. They not only convicted him of the rape; they determined that he was a criminal nuisance. The convictions carried several consecutive life sentences.

Lewis fondled the weapon in his hand—a dirk, fashioned like those of his accomplices in the prison machine shop. He had made the weapon from a sixty-penny nail. With painstaking attention, he had hand-honed it, buffed it, and sharpened it until it gleamed in the light. The spiny point was sharp enough to penetrate the mattress in his cell when he dropped it from a height of only six inches. He had faith it would impale human flesh like a hot knife through butter. A handgun would have been better for the task, but whether it was a bullet or a blade that left the lethal mark, dead was dead. And that was all that mattered.

The guard spoke as Lewis approached him. "Hey, Lewis, what's your problem? You ain't happy for your inmate buddy?"

Lewis didn't answer.

"Damn, Lewis. That sucks, not supporting one of your own kind."

Lewis's face turned deadly cold, but he felt a comforting warmth rush through his body. "I'll tell you, screw. Suck this!"

He slammed the dirk forward in a lightning-fast thrust. The needle-sharp point found the guard's throat and penetrated the back of his neck. The guard's eyes screamed his horror, but his voice didn't utter a sound. His open eyes saw nothing but darkness.

Lewis ran for the double doors and vanished into the night. Behind him, there was silence in the rec hall. The inmates, finally realizing what was going down, stood silent, emotionless as they looked around the rec hall at the four uniformed bodies. On the television, Caryn Collins sang her heart out in a touching country song. And for many of the inmates, because of the events of this night, Collins's song would forever be remembered as the Death Song.

———

She bowed in the spotlight, and the crowd went wild. Her star was shining brighter than even she had dreamed it could.

Inside, she was still the simple girl from a small town in southern Georgia. But so much had changed. When she stepped on the stage illuminated by the spotlights like some vestal angel and slid the microphone from its stand, the magic took control. And the fans—God, how she loved them. They were young and old, men and women, and they screamed, whistled, and cheered. They did it because they loved her. And they never let her forget it. But when the lights shone on her and her golden star glowed, she reciprocated that love with her powerful, captivating voice.

Caryn Collins had always been a dreamer. When she was a small child growing up in Georgia, she had lain awake at night and stared at the ceiling. Her imagination took control, and the tiny rays of light that streaked across the ceiling became the spotlights. And the sounds of the night pouring through the open window beside her bed became the applause. She lost herself in the imaginary patterns that danced before her eyes. She was the focus of the attention. She, Caryn Collins, was chosen . . . one of the very few whose star ascended above the rest with a golden glow. And when the images faded into darkness and her eyes closed in sleep, in her mind the dream danced on.

Someone had once told her in her early teenage years that it took only twenty years to become an overnight success. She laughed and tossed it off to negative thinking. In her mind, there was no room for anything that wasn't positive. If it didn't contribute to the dream or help it become reality, Caryn had neither the time nor the desire to be associated with it.

So here she stood, transmitting her magical splendor to another audience in another town. Caryn Collins, newly crowned Queen of Country Music. Just two days ago, her fans and peers had given her the crown at the Country Music Association Awards show. And although she was still in shock from the attention, she wore both the imaginary crown and the title proudly. Her coal-black hair sparked diamonds against the spotlights. One hundred and twelve pounds of smoking entertainment dynamite in a five-foot-seven-inch package. When the lights struck her hazel eyes, unending streaks of magic bounced back at the audience. She was, unquestionably, the new shining star of the 1990s.

When the night was over and the crowds had gone home, Caryn would board the tour bus and head for another town, another raving audience. Her voice haunted every place as she belted out the hits that had propelled her from southern Georgia to some galaxy far above anything she had known before.

The hit songs just kept coming. Caryn didn't always know where they came from, but they always came. If she didn't pen them herself, Bernie Aldridge, her manager and record producer, found them. There were touching songs, love songs, hard-hitting songs that captured the heart and soul of country fans around the world. And when her pen was dry, Bernie always knew where to find the next smash. And so it had been with her latest and perhaps her best recording to date. Bernie had suggested that they change a few lines in the song and a couple of notes in the melody. They could split the profits as co-writers.

An hour and forty-five minutes after the first blinding rays of the spotlight struck her, Caryn finished the show. There were three standing ovations and three encores. She molded the audience in the palm of her hand and played them all.

Another hour passed while she signed autographs, posed for photos and exchanged hugs and kisses with everyone from the mayor to factory workers and overweight housewives. It all came with the turf, and it fulfilled every expectation she had ever had about a shining star.

By the time Caryn had finished with the last camera-wielding fan, the road crew had torn down the stage set and loaded almost all the equipment into the eighteen-wheelers used to carry the sound and light support systems from show to show. The eight members of the band and backup vocalists had long since retired to the tour bus. By now, they were probably all asleep and waiting for the driver to get under way to the next city. They would sleep all night while miles of blacktop clicked away beneath them. When they got up somewhere around ten o'clock the following morning, they would be hundreds of miles away. And tomorrow night they would do it all again.

Caryn was exhausted by the time Bernie Aldridge joined her. He had finished his business with the show promoters and the civic-center manager. He carried a large bag with the night's receipts from consessions . . . photographs, T-shirts, baseball caps, and assorted souvenirs for which the fans so willingly handed over their hard-earned cash. He walked beside Caryn toward her private bus or as he called it, her land yacht. "Honey, you sure knocked 'em on their asses tonight. They must have bought thirty-five thousand dollars worth of goodies."

Caryn was tired and didn't feel like listening to Bernie get on one of his rampages about how much money they were making. "Bernie, I wish you wouldn't be so engrossed in the money all the time. There's a lot more to all this than money."

Aldridge laughed. "There is? Name something."

"Look, Bernie, I've told you this a thousand times. I do this because I love the people and I love my music. The money is secondary."

"Honey, that's why you've got me. And the money is why I've got you. Nothing lasts forever, darlin'. We've got to take all we can get while we can get it. You remember that."

"Bernie, you're a good manager and a great record producer, but one of these days your lust for money is gonna ruin you. Could you ever be happy just living life for the sake of living?"

Bernie laughed again. "Darlin', every time I think you've arrived on a level even with your success, you say something sweet and naive like that. Face it, love, without the money, what's the reason to live?"

Caryn shook her head in disgust, although she was smiling. "Bernie, honey, you're impossible. I'm glad you're on my side. I guess with seven number-one records . . . what can I say?"

"Say nothing at all, love, just keep singing like you do, and I'll take care of everything else."

Caryn climbed the steps onto the bus and Bernie followed. The engine idled while the driver secured the cargo doors. Bernie tossed the cloth money sack onto a seat in the front of the custom show bus. He fumbled through his pockets for a cigarette, lit it, and took a deep draw. "Ah, next stop, Cedar Rapids, Iowa, and another screaming crowd. I love it."

Caryn walked to the back of the bus and her private suite. Suddenly she stopped. She couldn't scream, but what she saw scared her worse than she had ever been scared in her life. There was a man there, and he had a gun pointed straight at her. She backed up one step at a time until she bumped into Bernie, who was facing the other way. He turned, startled. "What the—?"

The man with the gun spoke with an ice-tinged voice. "I'll do the talking, man. You do the listening. Got that?"

Bernie felt the blood flush from his head. "Who the hell are you?"

"You mean you didn't recognize my voice, Mister Bernie Aldridge? Your memory ain't for shit. Maybe the name will ring some bells for you. I'm Richie Halloway."

CHAPTER TWO

Marc Lee waited in line at the checkout of the little south Dallas convenience store. The highway warrior had noticed the man when he came in, so he had stalled for time and pretended to be looking at a magazine. But now the man was in front of him in line. The guy was Hispanic and probably not more than nineteen or twenty years old. He looked as if he had been pried from the crust of the earth with a crowbar. The kid's face was acne-scarred and weathered. But it wasn't just his looks that bothered Marc. It was the guy's right hand that never left his jacket pocket and the way he had scanned every face in the store. Maybe it was just a gut feeling, but Marc had learned long ago to listen to his gut—his instincts. Every time he had ignored them, he had regretted it.

Marc waited. The line slowly dwindled as the clerk behind the counter checked out the purchases and deposited the money in the cash register. There were only two people in front of the Hispanic man now. Marc noticed that the hard-looking man seemed unusually nervous. He kept shifting his weight from one foot to the other, then back again. He was fumbling around in his jacket pocket with his right hand. He carried a six-pack of beer in his left hand.

Another customer finished checking out and left the store. Marc could see the man getting more nervous by the minute.

The highway warrior snapped his fingers and turned from the line. "Forgot the potato chips," he said for the benefit of the nervous man. He walked across the store and found cover behind a display shelf of canned goods. Marc pretended to be looking for something on the shelf as the seconds clicked by like hours.

At last, the next customer finished paying and left the store. The Hispanic man was next. He was so nervous now that Marc thought he could see him tremble. The man faced the clerk. "Gimme a pack of Winstons, man."

"A dollar thirty-five for the cigarettes and three-ninety five for the beer. What else?" the clerk asked.

"Nothin', man." He handed the clerk a five-dollar bill and waited for his change.

The clerk handed him his change and the Winstons. The guy pocketed the money in his left pants pocket, picked up his brown paper bag, and turned away from the checkout counter. His right hand was still concealed in his jacket pocket, but he made no unusual movements.

"Maybe I misjudged this one," Marc mumbled to himself. But, for insurance, he reached beneath his light-weight jacket and gently slid the safety tumbler upward on his Smith & Wesson 5906 9-mm automatic.

The Hispanic took four steps away from the service counter. Behind him, the next customer stepped in front of the clerk. In a heartbeat, the Hispanic spun around. He jerked his right hand free of his pocket and produced a small chrome-plated automatic. He yelled as loudly as he could. "Okay, you mothers, this is a stickup! Move and I blow your friggin' brains out!" He waved the gun frantical-ly, motioning with it toward three people in the line and the clerk. "You three mothers get facedown on the floor. You gimme shit and I kill you."

The customers were panic-stricken. One by one they obeyed the gun-wielding man.

The shooter spun the gun around and stuck it into the clerk's face. "Ah-kay, dickface, gimme all the money from the register. No shit, man. Do what I tell you, and I will not hurt you. Screw me, man, and I splatter your brains. Move fast!"

"Don't hurt me. Take anything you want, but don't hurt anybody. It ain't worth it." The clerk was scared out of his mind. He opened the electronic cash register and jerked money from it as fast as he could. He took the twenties out first, and that triggered a silent alarm to the police department.

The gunner was shaking now. "Put it in a paper sack, man. Hurry!"

The clerk reached for a paper sack and crammed the money into it.

Marc carefully surveyed the situation. He slipped down behind the cover of the display rack and waited.

The robber was frantic. He waved the little chrome handgun erratically. His face had broken into a cold sweat. Beads of perspiration trickled across his acne scars and dropped from his cheeks. "Gimme the bag, man. Do it now! Quit screwin' around or I start killin' people. You hear me? Move!"

The clerk behind the counter was shaking so badly he couldn't talk. He shoved the bag of money forward on the counter.

The gunman reached for it, the muzzle of the little handgun waving all around the store. The muzzle finally settled in the direction of the clerk, and a shot echoed through the store. The resonant roar was muted by screams from the people on the floor. The bullet whizzed past the clerk's head and crashed into a cigarette display rack behind him. The clerk fell to the floor.

The gunman's hand wrapped around the bag. He jerked it from the counter and ran for the door.

Outside in the store parking lot, Carl Browne, Marc Lee's truck-driving companion in a never-ending war on crime, had jerked to full alert at the sound of the gunshot. He sat in one of the highway warrior's two highly customized and armored high-tech Jeep Cherokees. With the window down, the shot had sounded as if it were right beside him. Browne slumped down in the front seat of the Jeep and came out with his Smith & Wesson 5906 9-mm automatic. He glued his eyes to the front doors of the market. His senses shot to full-alert with the adrenaline rush. His heart raced because he knew Marc Lee was in that store, and the shot definitely wasn't from Marc's 9-mm.

The gunman was three steps away from the door when Marc came up from behind the display rack. The

Smith & Wesson had cleared leather from his hip holster, and he held it steadily in his right hand. The Novak three-dot combat sights lay aligned squarely in the middle of the gunman's back between the shoulder blades. "Stop or die!" Marc yelled.

The Hispanic man hesitated just long enough to look back and fire one more shot. The bullet from the little weapon went wild and hit a back wall of the store. He was through the doors and out of the store in two more running steps.

Marc cleared the cover of the display rack and ran for the door behind the fleeing robber.

Carl activated all of his mental senses when the second shot rang out. He sat poised for a firefight, the Smith & Wesson ready for action. He saw the bandit burst through the doors, and there was no mistaking him. He held the little automatic in one hand and a brown paper bag in the other, his face chiseled in fear. The man hit the parking lot on a dead run. The shooter didn't see Carl in the Jeep. He ran directly between the Cherokee and a Chevy pickup truck parked beside it.

Carl reacted quickly. The gunman was at the front fender of the Jeep when Carl jerked the Jeep's door handle with his left hand. He slammed it forward and completely open in one massive shove with his mighty forearm. The shooter couldn't react soon enough. The door hit him full-body with the force of a stationary brick wall. The money bag and the little handgun flew from limp fingers, one in one direction and the other in another, as he fell to the pavement.

Carl was out of the Jeep in a millisecond. He held the 9-mm automatic in a two-handed grip at arm's length, pointed at the shooter's bleeding face.

Marc burst through the doors just in time to see Carl level the Smith's muzzle at the bandit. "Nice work," he said as he stopped beside Carl. "How'd you know?"

Carl laughed. "I'm not deaf, and it's not the Fourth of July. What went down in there?"

"Wonder boy here must have needed a little dope money. You sure turned his switch off. What did you do?"

"Nailed his ass with the door when he ran between the vehicles. He never knew what hit him."

"I like that. I'll get a couple of nylon restraints, and we'll leave his ass for the boys in blue. I'd just as soon not be here when they come."

"I'll second that."

Marc walked to the Jeep and retrieved two nylon disposable handcuffs. He returned to Carl and the unconscious man. He rolled the shooter over and strapped his hands behind his back, then his ankles together. He placed the money bag and the little chrome pistol beside the man. "Let's hit it, bro."

"Let's." Carl dropped the safety tumbler on the Smith and got back in the Jeep.

Marc did likewise.

Carl had started from the parking lot when Marc looked at the microcomputer screen on the console of the Cherokee. "When did that come across?"

"What?"

"That message."

"I didn't see or hear anything. Must have linked in while we were playing back there. What's it say?"

"It says to contact Leeco Freight Lines immediately. Emergency situation. Urgent."

———

Shannon O'Connall was more than a little disgusted. This was the third time in as many months that he had stood before the same jailer, at the same window, for the same reason. Jails weren't foreign to him by any means, although he did appear out of place in the sea of police uniforms and one-piece fluorescent orange inmate jumpsuits. His custom-tailored three-piece pinstripe suit was about as inconspicuous as a shark's fin in a bathtub. But, as one of St. Louis's most noted and respected criminal defense attorneys, Shannon felt he had to uphold the image of standing just a little taller than the crowd.

Shannon exemplified the image well. His hands were smooth and soft. His nails were manicured and, as always, his black hair was groomed to perfection with nary a hair out of place. The *look* was dual-purpose: First, it served to intimidate those less fortunate than he was; second, it kept him in the good graces of the judges. And it didn't hurt that three of the judges he appeared before most often were silent partners in the exclusive men's clothing store where most of his wardrobe was purchased. After all, in a courtroom, it was the little, seemingly insignificant things that won or lost cases. And more than anything else besides going to the bank, Shannon O'Connall liked to win.

Then there was Roy, his older brother. And that was the reason he was here again today. Many times over the years, Shannon had seriously wondered if perhaps there had been an unfortunate mistake thirty-two years before at the hospital. Maybe somebody screwed up, and Captain and Mrs. O'Connall had gone home with the wrong baby. That, for lack of any other logical explanation, would explain a lot. And there were times when Shannon wanted a lot of explanation. It bugged him. Things like why everyone in the family had coal-black hair except Roy. His hair was auburn red. Everyone enjoyed getting a good summer suntan except Roy. He always burned and baked. Everyone in the family was self-motivated and ambitious except Roy. Their father was a retired army major. Their mother held a masters degree in economics. He held a law degree. But not Roy. No, Roy had dropped out of law school. The entire O'Connall family was mild-mannered and easygoing... except Roy. He had been an all-state quarterback during high school and that, Shannon thought, had jarred his brain. He also enjoyed getting his brains jarred in another way. He was an undefeated Golden Gloves middleweight champion. It didn't add up, and for years, Shannon had tried to convince himself that Roy was simply different. His pace was marked by a different rhythm, and his brain was on its own wavelength. Whatever the cause, the effect was that Roy had more recently become a royal pain in the ass.

It had been two days since Shannon's secretary had given him the message from Roy that asked him to get him out of jail. Shannon had decided he was quite busy, so he hadn't rushed to the county lockup to post his brother's bond. As a matter of fact, had it not been for the telephone call this morning from one of his most frequent clients, he would probably have just let old Roy serve his thirty days and be done with it. Marty Lucas at Interstate Leasing Services had changed that attitude. For all of his inadequacies, peculiarities, and bad habits, there was one thing that Roy O'Connall was the very best at: Catching crooks.

Shannon wasn't sure just how or why, but Roy was the best damned investigator he had ever seen. In the five years that Shannon had used him on a multitude of cases, Roy had batted a thousand. He solved them all and solved them quickly. And that in itself had started rumbles of a reputation for the unorthodox, redheaded O'Connall.

And now Shannon needed him. That was the only reason he was submitting himself to the personal embarrassment of standing before the jailer one more time. He had paid the fine for Roy's assault on a police officer, conferred with the judge, and secured the release of the weapon Roy had been charged with carrying illegally; now he stood stone-faced while a jailer went to the rear of the lockup to bring the unremorseful Roy to the threshold of freedom.

Roy stepped through the lockup door. "Well, brother, good to see you. Of course, it took you long enough. I've had to eat the slop they call food here for the last two days. Where the hell you been?"

Shannon remained stone-faced. "Don't push your luck, or I might change my mind."

"Hey, I love you too."

"Trust me, Roy, I wouldn't be here if I didn't have a case for you. It's the only way I'll ever get my money back."

"Now, Shannon, whatever happened to brotherly love and family loyalty and shit like that?"

"You happened to it, Roy. Need I say more?"

Roy took it on the cuff and forced a plastic smile. "Oh."

"Here, take your belongings, and let's get out of here before I reconsider my generosity."

"I'm right behind you."

Shannon turned and walked to the doorway leading

out of the jail. He shook his head and mumbled to himself as he reached the door. "Why does that bother me?"

They reached the parking lot behind the jail and stopped beside Shannon's solid black Mercedes 450 SL. Shannon deactivated the alarm and unlocked the door. He worked the electric-lock switch and got in the driver's seat. Roy made himself comfortable on the passenger's side.

Roy didn't waste any time getting to the meat of the matter. "Okay, brother. So what's your case?"

"In due time. First, I used some favors getting your sorry ass out of there this time. Dammit, Roy, I've told you about this a dozen times. All you'd have to do to get a permit to carry that damned gun is go down to the courthouse and make an application. You know it would be approved on my word alone. But no, not Roy O'Connall, hell, no. You have to go around on some kind of one-man crusade protesting about how unfair and unconstitutional the gun-permit business is. You just can't leave well enough alone. Three times I've had to come get your ass out of jail in the last three months. And do you care? Shit, no. Do you show me your thanks by going to get the permit? No! And this time—this time, you push it too far. You coldcock some cop when he's trying to put the cuffs on you, get charged with resisting arrest and assaulting a police officer. Now I admit the cop in question has a reputation of being an asshole, but that doesn't matter. For right now, the son of a bitch still wears a badge. You've got to respect that because I'm running out of favors and I'm damned tired of embarrassing myself to get you out of jail. Do you hear me?"

Roy just sat in the seat, his right elbow propped on his knee, his chin on his right fist. "You finished yet?"

"Hell, no, I'm not finished. One more incident like this, and I don't care how good you are, you're finished. Read my lips, Roy O'Connall. One more time, and *you are finished*! One more time, and I'll leave your ass to rot. Do you hear me?"

"You're cute when you're mad. You must get it from Mother's side of the family. What's the case that's so important that you would step from the golden portals of legal justice to free your insubordinate, ungrateful brother?"

"Damn! Why do I subject myself to this? Why?"

Roy raised his right index finger. "I can answer that. Matter of fact, you answered that. It's because I'm so damned good at what I do. Is that the right answer?"

Shannon exhaled hard and reached into his portfolio for a manila file folder. He pulled it out and opened it. He took two photographs from the folder and handed them to Roy. "These are photographs of two tour buses. They are the property of Interstate Leasing Service. They were leased to a country-music entertainer. Her name is Caryn Collins."

Roy took the photographs and looked at them carefully. "So? Is she behind on her payments, or what?"

"Just behind. Four days ago, Caryn Collins won a string of awards from the Country Music Association. Two nights ago, she was appearing in North Platte, Nebraska, on a show date. No one has seen her or the buses since then."

"So, how do you know she isn't just taking a little R and R?"

"Nope, not Caryn Collins. She's straight and a hard worker. She's one hundred percent dedicated to her work. Her payment record on the lease is flawless. Until yesterday, she had never even been late for a show date, much less missed one. Since the night in North Platte, no one has seen her or anyone in her road support team. The leasing company called us in as kind of a whim. It's a justified way to get involved. For the record, they want their buses back. For real, they want to know where Caryn Collins is and why she disappeared. Can you handle it?"

"Don't see why not. Face it, where do you hide a pair of buses?"

"We suspect someone knows the answer, and that's what our client is paying you to find out. On the surface, it appears she and her entire entourage may have been kidnapped."

"No shit? Sounds like somebody is pretty ambitious, wouldn't you say?"

"Yes. Collins has failed to appear for two show dates. One yesterday and one today. Her management company hasn't heard from her, nor has her record company. Find her, and find those tour buses."

"What else can you tell me about this broad?"

"Everything I know and everything I have been able to assemble in the last few hours is in this folder. I have current photographs, road-crew names, band names, backup-singer names, the works. All total, there are nineteen people, two buses, and two eighteen-wheelers that seem to have vanished from the face of the earth. It's your job to find them."

"What's it pay?"

Shannon smiled for the first time since he had arrived at the jail. "Your freedom and expenses—less attorney's fees of course."

Roy took the folder and grinned. "Of course. By the way, did I ever tell you I hate lawyers?"

CHAPTER THREE

Richie Halloway smoked the last cigarette from a pack he had taken from one of Caryn Collins's road crew. He balled up the empty pack and tossed it across the farmhouse floor. He knew he would have to make the pleasure of the last cigarette linger until tomorrow when he would send one of his accomplices into town for supplies. In the two days they had been at the farm, the intrusion of twenty-four people had taken its toll on the food stock. They had eaten everything on the buses and most of what Lilly Arthur had stored in her pantry.

When he thought of Lilly Arthur, Halloway almost laughed. He thought the old woman was going to keel over and die when she saw Ray Hartley. He was like a demonic ghost from her past. The old woman farmer turned a half-dozen shades of pale when she recognized his face. Hartley loved it. During his years in confinement, the killer of the woman's husband and daughter had decided to torment the old woman just a bit before he punched her ticket. The arrival of Caryn Collins and her complete entourage was sufficient torment in itself, but Ray Hartley wanted more to satisfy his whims.

In the weeks before the escape, when Halloway and Hartley had talked, Richie thought it would be brilliant to use the farm in northern Nebraska as a hiding place until he gained what he sought from Caryn Collins and Bernie Aldridge. After all, with miles and miles of fields, rolling hills, and little population, upstate Nebraska was made to order for his deed of retribution. Even if the authorities had an inkling where he was, it would take a small army to

21

find him. And if they happened to get lucky and come close, Richie had an alternate plan for that also. He would simply kill Bernie Aldridge and Caryn Collins, and be done with it. Then the slate would be clean, or better yet, he would be ahead.

The tour buses and the eighteen-wheelers he had commandeered from Collins and company fit quite well into the large barn that had sat mostly empty until his arrival. And with the Collins entourage securely corralled into one large room in the old frame house, Halloway felt comfortable that he and his friends had everything under control. That was just the way he liked it.

When he sent one of his people into town tomorrow, he would be sure to get enough food to last at least a week. Of course, money was no longer an object. Bernie Aldridge had seen to that, although perhaps unwillingly. Richie had found the receipts from the concert concession sales still in a cloth sack in a seat on the bus. The best he could guess, there was at least thirty or forty thousand dollars there. That would buy a hell of a lot of food and beer. Whatever was left would make a modest down payment on what he figured Aldridge owed him.

Everything was going according to plan. The escape had been far easier than he had expected. Once he and his people had disposed of the guards in the rec hall, there had been no other resistance. Thanks to Amy Markham, the driver of the bread-delivery truck who ran the route to the prison every day, the getaway from the facility had been the proverbial piece of cake. The escapees had simply loaded into the back of the stepvan truck, covered themselves with crates, and road right out the front gate. No one had been the wiser. Halloway almost felt guilty because it had been so damned easy.

Once they were away from the joint, Amy's van was waiting twenty-five miles away with everything Richie had ordered. There were exactly the weapons he wanted, the survival knives, clothing, food, and enough ammunition to make a good stand in a small war. When his game of vengeance was played out, he had a couple of friends from Omaha to whom he was deeply indebted. He was also indebted to the one who had financed his weaponry. He knew he would somehow see that they were all properly repaid. But first things first. And right now, Caryn Collins and Bernie Aldridge came first.

Halloway looked out a front window at the acres and acres of lush fields. It was a sight he had thought he would never see again. he felt the satisfaction of freedom, but he knew he would never again be really free. Even when this was all over, he knew, deep in the depths of his soul, that the unforgiving eyes of the law would never stop searching for him. Sooner or later they would find him and the others. That meant his time was limited, and it greatly narrowed his future options. It also narrowed the chance that Collins and Aldridge would ever leave the Nebraska farm alive.

Lionel Lewis came in from his post outside. He held a Remington 870 twelve-gauge riot shotgun at his side. "Hey, Richie, my man, what's the plan?"

Halloway tossed the remnants of the cigarette into the stone fireplace. "We just cool it until tomorrow. I want one volunteer to take the van and go into town. We need more supplies. You know, man, groceries and shit like that. I want some beer so we can have a party. I think we need to celebrate. What do you think, Lionel?"

"Hell, yes. I can dig me some of that. I been eyeing that black chick that sings with the white bitch. Me and her, hey, we might just have our own little party." Lewis laid the shotgun on a sofa and sat down. He cupped his hand around his crotch and laughed.

"Lionel, my man, you're too bad. You really are."

"Hey, Rich, what are we gonna do with all of these people? Them roadies are gettin' to be a pain in the ass. I don't think they like us too much."

"Tolerance, Lionel. We need 'em all right now for bargainin' chips. When the need is gone, they're gone. We get a little closer to what we're after, and we can shed some of the excess baggage. Whaddaya think?"

"Yeah. I like it, man."

"Okay, look here. I want to talk to Collins now. Me and her, you see. I got a few things I gotta get off my chest. You know, straighten out. Why don't you go in there and bring her to me, huh?"

"Sure, Rich. My pleasure." Lewis stood and grabbed

his shotgun. He went to the other side of the living room and disappeared into a hallway. When he reached the room he wanted, he knocked three times and waited for the proper response from inside.

Cliff Scott knocked on the door twice from the other side and then opened it. Lewis went in. He scanned the faces of their captives. Most appeared either bored or dejected. Most except Lilly Arthur. She looked somewhere between dead and terrified. Lewis locked his eyes on Caryn Collins, who sat beside Bernie Aldridge on a small love seat. Her eyes locked with his, and she blushed. Lewis smiled. "Come on, white bitch. Somebody wants to talk to you."

Collins hesitated. She felt her heart race and the veins in her temples pound. Her normally strong voice was trembling when she finally gathered the nerve to answer. "Who, me?"

Lewis's voice was cold and impassionate. "Come on, don't play dumb with me. Who the hell else would I be talkin' to if I'm lookin' at you? Get your pretty ass up and come with me."

Collins looked at Aldridge as if she were seeking the authority to move. He nodded his head, and she got up from the love seat. She adjusted her tight-fitting jeans and pulled her blouse down until it covered her hips. "Who wants to see me?"

"Richie."

Aldridge stood. "What does he want?"

Lewis leveled the shotgun at Aldridge. "I guess that ain't a damned bit of your business, Mr. Boss Man. Set your ass down before I blow it off."

Aldridge was stunned. He looked hard at Lewis, then at the shotgun. He sat down.

Collins walked to the door and waited for Lewis to open it.

Lewis looked at Scott and winked. "See you in a few, dude. Keep 'em cool."

Scott glanced around the room, then looked back at Lewis. "Yeah, my man. Ain't no sweat. They're cool."

Lewis opened the door and nudged Caryn Collins into the hallway with the barrel of the Remington shotgun.

Richie Halloway was waiting when Lewis came back

with Caryn Collins. At the moment, she looked like any other human being. There was nothing on the surface that separated her from any other attractive woman he had ever known. He looked into her eyes. Behind the fear, he saw a woman who, given another time and other circumstances, would probably be a compassionate and loving person. "Hello, Caryn. Please have a seat. I want to talk to you."

"Talk? You've taken me from my work, and you're holding my entire entourage against our will. What could I possibly have to talk to you about?"

"Spirited. I like that in a woman. I have something I want you to read into this tape recorder." Halloway handed a small cassette tape recorder to Collins and then a piece of paper.

Collins took the recorder and the paper. She read over the paper and spit fire at Halloway with her eyes. "And what happens if I refuse to read it?"

"Oh, that's simple. I just start early."

Caryn's face flushed. She sat the recorder on a coffee table and pushed the buttons to record. She held the paper at arm's length and read. "This is Caryn Collins. This is not a joke or a prank. My band and my road crew and I have been taken hostage because of something my manager did. I can't tell you what it is now. That will come later. I want everyone to know that all of us are okay. My captors will have certain demands that will follow soon. In the meantime, this message is for the executives of my record company and my management company. You must prepare three million dollars in small bills to be paid as part ransom. You will receive instructions as to what must be done with the money in a day or two. If you do not comply with the demands of my captors, they will kill one member of my band or road crew for every twelve hours you fail to comply."

Collins stopped reading and stared at Halloway. Her voice mellowed, and she looked frightened. "Are you serious about this?"

Halloway's face was cold and expressionless. "Every single word of it."

Marc made the telephone call on the cellular telephone as soon as Carl straightened the Cherokee out on the street, but the information was sketchy at best. He'd told the receptionist at Leeco that he and Carl would be at the terminal in a little under fifteen minutes. His estimate had been liberal because it took only ten before Carl wheeled the Cherokee into the fenced lot at Leeco.

Winston Andrews was waiting for the highway warriors when they entered the terminal. Andrews was usually a reserved man who managed to show little emotion. His head was mostly bald; the few remaining strands of hair were a mixture of black and gray. Winston was slightly overweight, his pudgy cheeks etched with red streaks from superficial blood veins. Marc never recalled seeing him smile. He suspected that if he ever did see the quiet man smile, Winston's face might shatter between the red lines and crumble to the floor. But personality aside, Winston Andrews was a damned efficient man at what he did. He was one of several people placed in key positions at Leeco by the President of the United States when Marc and Carl had agreed to the business proposition the President had presented them. And that had been—how long ago? Marc wasn't sure, but it seemed that a couple of lifetimes had passed since he and Carl took the Big Man up on his offer.

Andrews was an accountant by profession. His duty at Leeco was overseer of financial affairs. In essence, all bucks stopped at Winston Andrews's desk. He ran Leeco, on the books at least, as if it were his own.

Marc knew that when his father, Marcus Lee, awakened from the dark sleep induced by an edged weapon in the hands of Rafaello Segalini's mob at the beginning of the never-ending war on crime, the elder Lee would be pleased at the financial progress of Leeco Freight Lines. The terminal had been rebuilt since fire destroyed it and bombs exploded around it in another battle to rid the country of criminal scum. Winston Andrews had done a top-notch job of managing Leeco, and Marc longed for the day when he could tell his father all about it.

Marc offered his hand to Andrews. "What's up, Winston?"

Winston accepted the hand. "Maybe nothing, maybe

something big. I'm not too sure. We got a call just a little while ago from an attorney in St. Louis by the name of Shannon O'Connall. O'Connall represents one of the largest leasing companies in the country for heavy equipment. It's called Interstate Leasing Service, out of Houston. O'Connall says that Interstate has a lease agreement with a country-music entertainer by the name of Caryn Collins."

Marc interrupted. "I know Caryn Collins. Well, I should say my father knows Caryn. He was involved with her early in her career. That was several years ago. He invested some money as I recall."

"Hum, well, I didn't know about that, but Leeco is involved with Caryn Collins. I'll get to that in a moment. Anyway, O'Connall says that Interstate contacted him and requested his assistance in locating Collins and her touring entourage. Interstate leased the tour buses Collins uses to travel to her various show dates around the country."

Marc wasn't sure he understood what Andrews was getting at. "Help me a little. What's the Leeco tie-in?"

"I'm coming to that. Collins hasn't been heard from for two days. Matter of fact, no one in her entire traveling company has been heard from. It's got a lot of people worried. Catch is, Collins is one of these people who prides herself on promptness. Apparently, she's never even been late for a dental appointment, if you catch what I'm saying."

Marc forced a grin. "Go on."

"Well, Collins has simply disappeared. She did a show in North Platte, Nebraska, two nights ago. After the show was over and the troupe departed the venue, they seemed to vanish from the face of the earth."

Marc shook his head. "Did I miss something, or did you not mention what that has to do with Leeco Freight Lines?"

"A lot. As part of her traveling road show, Collins needed the use of two eighteen-wheel over-road rigs to haul her sound, lights, and stage equipment. Those two rigs belong to Leeco. It's an agreement your father made several years ago. Collins's management company leases the rigs from Leeco."

"Okay, it's a little clearer now. But is she or her management company behind on the payments or something? How do we fit in?"

"Oh, no, nothing like that. Quite the contrary. The payments are made annually. They're paid through the end of the year, in advance."

"I'm lost. Help me again."

"Okay, this O'Connall guy wants our help in locating Collins and all of the equipment. Mostly Collins, though. From all indications, O'Connall thinks maybe Collins and her troupe have been kidnapped. This type of vanishing act is too uncharacteristic of Caryn Collins."

"Is O'Connall convinced this isn't some kind of sick publicity stunt?"

"Yeah, he says there are only a few people who know about her disappearance. They're trying to keep a lid on it for now. He insists that Collins doesn't need publicity. She was selected Entertainer of the Year four days ago, and her records are selling as fast as they can manufacture them. He thinks this is big-time trouble."

"Isn't this a job for the FBI?"

"Sure, if they knew for certain it was a kidnapping. O'Connall wanted us to notify him if we had any contact with anyone from Collins's organization. I take it that's what he meant when he said he needed our help."

Marc turned and looked at Carl. "What do you think, bro?"

Carl shrugged. "Might as well. We got a few days to kill. Nothin' big happenin' right now. I guess we should try to protect Leeco's interest and nose around a little. How 'bout you?"

"Yeah, might as well." Marc turned back to Winston Andrews. "Winston, can you get me everything you have on this so far? I'd like to place a telephone call to this Shannon O'Connall and chat with him. After that, if it appears warranted, Carl and I might take a trip up toward Nebraska and see how the wheat crops are faring."

"Good. I'll get the identification numbers from the file so you can positively identify the rigs should you happen to encounter them. I'll have all of this on a computer printout within thirty minutes. Is that soon enough?"

Marc nodded his head. "Yes, that will be fine. Could you get me Shannon O'Connall's telephone number before you start the other stuff?"

Andrews disappeared into his office and returned in less than a minute with the number Marc requested. He handed a slip of paper to Marc. "This should do it. Maybe O'Connall can give you a little more insight."

Marc took the paper and scanned over the number. "Great. I'll give Mr. O'Connall a call and see what he has to offer. I'd also like to know if my father has anything in his files about the truck lease or any other dealings he might have had with Caryn Collins. Can you do that for me?"

Andrews didn't hesitate. "Sure, no problem, Marc."

"Good. A little homework might save a lot of legwork. If Caryn Collins has really been kidnapped, it might also help save her life."

———

Bernie Aldridge got up from the love seat and moved around the room until he was beside Mike Coble. Coble, the Caryn Collins Show road manager, stood with his arms crossed, looking out the only window in the room. His back was toward Cliff Scott, who guarded the door with some kind of small weapon that Aldridge thought resembled a submachine gun.

Coble was a giant man in his late twenties. He stood at least six-four, and his weight matched the height. There was one deception to his appearance—his hair. He had lost most of it when he was only twenty-two. He laughed about his shiny scalp and took this unfortunate twist of nature with good humor. He said that some men became prematurely gray, but he had avoided the middle-aged rush and gone directly to prematurely bald. Coble was soft-spoken and normally quite shy. He had worked for Caryn Collins since she formed her first road crew four years earlier. As the chief roadie, it was his responsibility to see that all the technical loose ends were securely tied before every performance. When the show was over, Coble supervised the takedown process and saw to it that everything was loaded back into the eighteen-wheelers for the trip to the next one-night stand. In the time he had worked for Collins, Coble had developed an infallible system for the setup and takedown procedures. They day-in-day-out routine of lifting heavy stage risers, light pods, and sound-mixing boards had caused Coble to build huge muscles in his arms and legs. Except that he was mostly bald, Coble resembled a big bear. His nature, however, was more that of a lamb—until someone pissed him off.

Mike Coble was very pissed off.

Bernie rested his arms on the windowsill beside Coble. He spoke softly, barely above a whisper, so Scott couldn't hear. "What are you thinking, Mike?"

"Gotta be a way out of here without gettin' anybody hurt, Bernie. There's only five of these shitheads, and there's nineteen of us."

"I can't argue with that. Trouble is, they got the guns."

"Not all of 'em."

"What?"

"I've got a nine millimeter automatic in my toolbox on the number-one bus."

"Humm. A hell of a lot of good that does us in here."

"I'll come up with a way. Give me a little time. You got any idea what this is all about, Bernie?"

"Yes and no. I think it involves Caryn's latest song. I also think these guys are prison escapees. If that's the case, we may be in serious trouble."

"I think that is an understatement. We're already in serious trouble. I don't even know where we are, do you?"

"Somewhere in Nebraska. That's all I know. They seemed to know exactly where they were taking us when we came here. That's interesting."

Coble took a deep breath and then exhaled. "If I can get to my gun, I can take one or two of 'em before they know what's hit 'em. That could instantly lower the odds and get us more firepower. I think we can get out of this, Bernie. But I gotta get to my gun. There's gotta be a way."

Bernie nodded his head slightly. "Maybe there is."

CHAPTER FOUR

Roy O'Connall wasn't particularly fond of the crap he had to take from his brother. There were times when he thought it might be more advantageous to spend the menial time in jail rather than listen to the holier-than-thou lectures Shannon invariably had in store for him. His latest escapade was one of those times. And besides, Roy was damned convinced that his arrest had been unwarranted. He was simply trying to help a lady friend in need.

Mistake number one: Beware of lady friends in need. It had all sounded so normal when she told him that an old boyfriend was hassling her. Roy, good guy that he was, set out to rescue the fair damsel in distress from the jaws of the fire-breathing dragon.

Mistake number two: Mind your own business unless the price is right. In this case, the price wasn't right. Matter of fact, there wasn't even a price. It was a freebie.

Mistake number three: Always get *all* of the facts before you run headlong into the symbolic brick wall. What the lady friend had neglected to tell him was that the old boyfriend was also a cop.

Mistake number four (the clincher): Never go around trying to beat the hell out of a cop, even if he's hassling a lady friend in distress. They're mean and dangerous underneath the deceptive lambskin so many of them wear. More importantly, never go around trying to beat the hell out of a cop when carrying a weapon for which you have neglected to obtain a permit, lest the jaws of a pair of Smith & Wesson handcuffs clamp their metallic teeth into your wrists.

31

Roy reasoned that hard-learned lessons were the lessons learned best. With the error of his ways safely stored in his mental computer, O'Connall made himself a vow that he would not make the same mistakes again. Time to chalk it up to experience and get down to the task before him: Caryn Collins.

Shannon had such a way of presenting the next case to Roy. Roy, however, attributed it to the fact that Shannon was an attorney. If there was one thing he had absorbed through the years, it was that attorneys were long on judgments and short on diplomacy. Shannon was no exception, brother or not. The second thing he had learned about attorneys was that they were exceptionally proficient at grasping one's testicles and placing them in a vise. Once they had your nuts in a bind, they sure as hell knew how to squeeze. Again, Shannon was no exception.

Roy decided that, like AIDS, the clap, and married women, attorneys were best avoided when at all possible . . . especially if the attorney was your brother.

Caryn Collins.

According to the file Shannon had furnished, the goods on Caryn Collins and her rising career from little Miss Nobody to superstar were too squeaky clean. The story of her rise to superstardom lingered somewhere between fantasy and reality. The file read something like a bedtime story where the shabbily clad little girl is kissed by the handsome prince and is magically in control of her queendom. Nothing was out of place. And that, Roy knew, wasn't right. No way—at least not in the entertainment business of the 1990s.

Roy knew enough from his limited experience with entertainers to know that superstars weren't born, they were made. They were manufactured products of concept, organization, promotion, and marketing. Although that wasn't the kind of thing dream bubbles were made of, it was the *real* bottom line. Manufactured products of someone's imagination—nothing more, nothing less. The "star" was the delivery system for creative expertise. He also knew that for every smile in front of the audience or the camera, there were a thousand tears when the crowds were gone and the lights turned off. It was a game of imagery where some guy with a knack for finding voids spotted a vacancy and filled it with the product of his ingenuity.

That took him to the problem. With Caryn Collins, all of the tracks leading to her hallowed golden-girl glow were void of the behind-the-scenes trappings normally associated with a star rising at the speed of a meteorite. And that scared the hell out of him because that deduction itself meant he would have to dig quite deep to find all the skeletons. Excavations in a potentially lethal case took time, and any time lost could be at the expense of human life.

Roy O'Connall ran the scenario through his mind. The first question to register was Who would have something to gain if Caryn Collins was no longer among the living? The second question was What if the intended target wasn't Caryn Collins at all? What if it was someone in her entourage? Worse yet, what if the kidnapping, if indeed there had been a kidnapping, was perpetrated to gain some sick retribution for someone in one of Collins's many support organizations? The possibilities self-generated at the speed of a carcinogenic bacterium. With someone who had achieved the sudden stature of Caryn Collins, the intended targets could be endless. There were booking agencies; management, record, and promotion companies; distribution networks; publicity companies; leasing companies; the list ran on and on. Roy decided the best place to start was whichever place he could get to first.

O'Connall pulled an atlas from his attaché case and thumbed through it. He flipped to the two-page map of the United States. It didn't take a genius to figure out that it was a lot closer from St. Louis to Nashville than it was to central Nebraska. But then there was the logical side of the coin to consider. Logic said that Caryn Collins didn't disappear from Nashville. She disappeared from central Nebraska. Although there might be leads in Nashville, the trail, if she had left one, that led from North Platte to wherever Collins and the buses were now was growing colder with each passing minute. A supersleuth would probably start in Nashville, at the roots. From there, he could either build a motive and establish a potential trail or clear the slate of numerous suspects. Why? Because it was the reasonable thing to do.

Roy closed the atlas and tossed it on the seat. He slammed the Corvette into gear and headed for North Platte, Nebraska.

———

Ray Hartley walked through the old Nebraska farmhouse. Memories swarmed through his mind like a swarm of bees. And the stings were just as painful. He had relived it all in the time he had been at the farm. It kept playing over and over in his mind like the songs on the radio the first night he made love to her in the backseat of his '67 Chevy.

Mary Beth Arthur. He had loved her more than life itself. Her soft skin. Her sun-streaked brown hair. Her dazzling blue eyes. Two Nebraska farm kids finding love and life in the backseat of a beat-up old Chevrolet on isolated dusty backroads that led nowhere. But that high school romance led to more. Much more.

Harold Arthur was a big-time beef farmer. His farm covered some of the nicest acreage in the Big Sands area of north-central Nebraska. It spanned slightly more than a thousand acres. He was a man driven by the fear of God and the sweat of his sunburned brow. He prided himself on being a simple, honest man who gave all he had to his wife, his child, and his land. In exchange for his gift of life and sustenance, he expected his family to adhere to the puritanical standards he so rigorously abided by.

Somehow, old Harold found out about the nights in the backseat. Or maybe he knew all along. Maybe Lilly, Mary Beth's mother, knew and she betrayed the trust. Anyway, old Harold flew into a fit of spiritual rage, damning and condemning Mary Beth and the farmboy who had deceived her into the submission that resulted in the loss of her virginity. He vowed she would never again lay eyes on the low-life source of her sin. That she was seventeen and possessed of an insatiable womanly yearning didn't matter. Harold ordered her never again to see or speak to the evil one who had deprived her of her purity. He made her drop to her knees before the eyes of God and beg for forgiveness. Then he made her solemnly vow to keep his command.

Mary Beth kept the vow about a week. Then her biological cravings overpowered her better judgment, and she slipped off to meet Ray Hartley. Both their needs were satisfied twice a week for about a month, and then old Harold found out again. And this time, when he finished beating the hell out of Mary Beth, he vowed to shoot the devil incarnate on sight.

Harold's demands accomplished little more than provide fuel for the flames of rebellion that burned in Mary Beth's heart. Another month passed with Ray and Mary Beth meeting often enough to satisfy their physical requirements.

And then, like a raging bolt of lightning from the overcast Nebraska sky, Mary Beth told Ray it was all over. The hell of it was that she waited until they had finished making love to break it to him. She never said why. All she said was that she didn't love him anymore.

Three weeks passed, and Ray Hartley existed day-to-day by sheer mechanics. He tried to call her. He sent her letters. He slipped to her house under the cover of darkness. She wouldn't change her mind and didn't reply to any of his pleas. Worse than anything else, she wouldn't give him a valid explanation. Until the day she died, she never told him why. And it was months later, at the trial, that he finally learned the truth.

Hartley went off the deep end. He decided to kill the man who had taken the only person he had ever loved. The only person he *could* ever love.

He laid his plan with the same cunning that a spider weaves his web. Armed with a broken heart and a .30-30 Winchester rifle, he set out on his course of destruction. On the first night of the full moon, he made his way to the Arthur farm. He found them all there—Mary Beth, Lilly, and Harold. He watched from outside. Lilly worked in the kitchen. Mary Beth was in her second-floor bedroom, propped up on her bed and reading a book. Harold sat in the living room in his favorite worn chair. Above him, the light of a floor lamp illuminated the pages of his Bible.

It was a known fact that people in the country or on the farms seldom if ever locked their doors. Most probably didn't even know where the key was, if they had ever had one. And that made it all the better.

Ray Hartley fed the Winchester's magazine until it was full. He worked the lever and jacked a round into the chamber. Then he carefully lowered the hammer until it reached the first cocknotch. He took a deep breath, stood from behind the cover of a sprawling grapevine, and made the first step that would change his life forever.

Even today, nine years later, Hartley could see the undiluted fear in the old man's eyes when the barrel of the Winchester came through the front door. Old Harold pressed back in his chair like he was glued to it. He dropped the Bible on his lap, still open, and barked out at Hartley. Ray had heard the words over and over a million times since that night: "Boy, what in the name of God do you think you're doing?"

Hartley even remembered his exact reply. "I've come for Mary Beth, and then I'm going to kill you."

The old farmer's eyes had gotten as big as saucers. He yelled for Mary Beth to come downstairs. She did.

Ray Hartley could still hear the sound of her footsteps coming from the second floor. And her voice . . . it kept ringing in his ears. The same pleading words. "Ray, please, no. This is not the way. Put that rifle down. Please, Ray."

And Hartley could still see Lilly Arthur step from the kitchen and stop at the living-room door. The puritanical old bitch was wiping her hands on an apron and reprimanding him at the same time. "Boy, have you lost your mind? You put that gun down and leave this house right now, or I'm calling the sheriff. I mean it, Ray."

That's when it all came apart. Lilly Arthur dropped her apron and reached for the telephone on a little table just inside the living room. When her hand touched the telephone, his finger squeezed the trigger.

Hartley stood at the living-room door now. He saw it all in slow motion. The hammer dropped on the rifle, and dust fell from the ceiling and walls from the thunderous report of the high-powered rifle. The 170-grain soft-pointed bullet slammed through Lilly Arthur's chest. The impact knocked her back into the kitchen. Blood splayed on the walls and slowly ran toward the floor. Lilly Arthur collapsed on the kitchen floor. He could still see her hand twitch, and then she stopped moving.

Even now, Hartley could hear the screams. In his mind, he could see it all again. Mary Beth ran toward him from across the room. Harold jumped from his chair, and the Bible sailed across the living-room floor. Harold was coming at him. And Mary Beth—she had the rifle barrel at just the instant he jacked the empty out and fed a fresh round into the chamber. Harold was there, swinging at him. He jerked back, tried to jerk the rifle free. It went off. Another thunderous roar of death vibrated the walls. And this time, the bullet missed its intended mark. Missed Harold. Instead, the soft-pointed death missile blew away Mary Beth's heart and left a gaping hole. The repercussions also shattered Ray Hartley's heart forever and annihilated any feelings of compassion he ever had.

And then he couldn't stop. He ejected the empty across the floor and jacked a new round into the chamber. Harold was screaming at him, but the screaming stopped with the third roar of thunder when Harold was only a foot from the rifle barrel.

He dropped to his knees. Mary Beth lay dead beside the open Bible. He took her into his arms, held her tightly, and stroked her hair. He gently laid her back on the floor. He looked at his hands and saw blood there. Her blood. And even today, when he looked into his open palms, he could see her blood on his hands, after all these years. That in itself was punishment enough for all he had done.

He had left the house and fled into the northern Nebraska hills. Two weeks later, a sheriff's posse caught him, and he sat for months in the county jail while Lilly Arthur healed from her wound.

At the trial, the medical examiner testified that Mary Beth Arthur was pregnant. Then, and only then, Ray Hartley knew why.

Lilly Arthur had somehow survived her wounds that night. This time she wouldn't.

Hartley came back to reality and opened the locked bedroom door where he had moved Lilly Arthur. Nine years ago, the room had been Mary Beth's bedroom. Today, it was Lilly Arthur's prison. The elderly woman's eyes radiated fear and hatred when she saw him. Hartley took the knife from the sheath on his hip and stroked it. He looked at Lilly and grinned a sardonic grin. "Soon, Lilly. Very soon."

The old woman didn't speak, but her breathing was visibly labored and she trembled.

Hartley felt a certain warmth from Lilly Arthur's terror, but he could still see the open Bible on the bloody floor beside Mary Beth's body. And the part he remembered most were the words that seemed to jump from the pages at him that night: *Thou shalt not kill*.

———

Marc's call to Shannon O'Connall had produced little more than Winston Andrews had already told him. The only tidbit Marc found useful was the fact that the leasing company that owned Caryn Collins's tour buses had hired a private investigator to "recover" the buses.

Andrews returned with the lease file. Marc took it and thumbed through it. Andrews had anticipated Marc's next request, a photocopy of the complete file for Marc to keep.

Carl Browne looked through the file also. When he was finished, he closed it and looked up at Marc. "Not much in here to point an accusatory finger. You think this case is legit, or is it a case at all?"

"Hard to say. Maybe it is and maybe it isn't. Not much happening around here. Since we've got a little time to kill, you want to go see Nebraska?"

Carl shrugged. "Why not?"

A young woman secretary knocked lightly on the door and stepped inside. "Excuse me, Mr. Lee."

Marc looked back at the door and the attractive young woman. "Yes?"

"Sir, you have a telephone call on line five. A Mr. Crain."

"Thank you." Marc pushed the button and picked up the receiver. "Marc Lee."

"Well, well, aren't we formal when in the presence of sexy voices? How the hell are you?"

"Brittin, I'm fine. And you?"

"Gettin' better by the day. What's happenin' in sweet-home Dallas?"

"Not much. You sound as if you've adjusted to the nation's capital."

"I have. Well, as much as anyone can adjust to this place. Listen, this isn't a call to exchange subtle pleasantries. The boss has something he wants you and Carl to look into. Can you get to a radio and contact me on ComSat-D? I'd rather pass this along on a scrambled network. You never know where the ears are. Catch my drift?"

Marc chuckled. "Yeah, old buddy, I catch it. Whatever you have must be heavy. Give me two minutes, and I'll call you from the Cherokee on ComSat-D. That okay?"

"Affirmative. Two minutes, and I'll be standing by for your call. See you."

"Right." Marc hung up and turned to face Carl. "Let's get to the Jeep and see what good news Brittin has." Marc was up from the desk and headed for the door.

Carl nodded and followed Marc to the door. Once outside, he broke the silence. "What's up?"

"Don't know. Brittin says he has something for us that he'd like to pass along over the scrambler. Telephones scare him . . . but that's understandable."

Carl shut off the alarm system and unlocked the Cherokee. He and Marc climbed in and closed the doors.

Marc made the radio call to Brittin Crain at the Justice Department in Washington, D.C. He keyed the microphone attached to the Icom IC-V100 transceiver. The radio instantly linked to the nationwide Defense Department radio repeater system and one of the numerous K-band transponders strategically located across the United States that linked into the ComSat-D earth-orbiting satellite. At the speed of light, the Jeep Cherokee parked in the parking lot at Leeco Freight Lines in Dallas, Texas, was in contact with Brittin Crain in Washington. Marc held the transmit button down as he spoke. "Barnburner, this is Pathfinder. Do you copy? Over." He released the black transmit switch on the side of the microphone.

The encode-decode system inside the Icom as well as in the ComSat-D satellite system functioned at a real-time rate of sixty times per second. In order to communicate with any radio transceiver in the system, the transceiver required an electronic *handshake*—a subroutine encode-decode initialization. Once the systems locked on to each other, the digital circuitry took control of the cryptic scrambling of the radio traffic. Should unwanted ears be tuned to the proper frequencies, and they usually were, all they could hear without the digital initialization was unintelligible, sharply garbled sound similar to a henhouse full of clucking chickens—all about an octave too high. For a properly equipped transceiver, there was little, if indeed any, loss of audio quality.

"Roger, Pathfinder. This is Barnburner. That was fast. Got some info for you. Are you ready to copy? Over."

"Roger, Barnburner. Go ahead with your traffic. We're ready."

A courtesy tone sounded on the repeater link, and Brittin's voice came from the speaker. "Okay, Pathfinder. Four nights ago, four men escaped from the Nebraska State Penitentiary after killing four guards. These men were all hard-types, and they were serving long sentences. I'll fill in the details in a minute or two. Up to the minute, the bureau can't find a trace of them. If you can activate your fax unit, I'll transmit a complete portfolio with photographs. Can you do that?"

Marc keyed the transceiver again. "Give me fifteen seconds and go to it, Barnburner. Over."

"Standing by."

Marc entered a sequence of numerals into the on-board computer and activated the radio fax unit in the customized over-road rig parked across the lot. He waited for a verification signal. It came, and then he heard the digital electronic transmission across the Icom's speaker. Five minutes later, the digital signal ended and was immediately followed by another verification tone from the Leeco rig's fax unit.

"Pathfinder, did you get all that?"

"Roger, Barnburner. All received. We'll go take a look in a couple of minutes."

"Okay, Pathfinder, but listen well. The boss wants your expertise on this one. I'll give you more later. Let that suffice for now. And one more thing. There's one of these guys that's real bad news. His name is Richie Halloway. The guy fancies himself a musician, but should you encounter him, be damned careful. When he's in the right frame of mind, his favorite tune is a death chant."

CHAPTER FIVE

Caryn Collins couldn't remember the last time she had cooked a meal. And breakfast at that. It seemed so long ago. Best she could recall, her last effort in the kitchen had been years ago when her dream of stardom had been little more than a fantasy. Not that she felt cooking was beneath her, but now her schedule was so busy, she had no time to practice her culinary artistry. But here she was, captive on an isolated Nebraska farm with a band of mentally twisted escapees, and she was standing over a frying pan waiting for the shortening to melt. Marilee Evans, a young backup singer in Caryn's road show, had made biscuits from scratch. Their tantalizing aroma drifted lazily from the oven and filled the old country kitchen with a smell that took Caryn back to her childhood. For a while, it masked the seriousness of their situation. Despite the circumstances and the hostility of the environment, Caryn thought being in the kitchen again felt good.

She cracked the eggs that one of the captors had brought in from a chicken house located somewhere in the farmyard. Caryn dropped the eggs into a shallow bowl, mixed them, and beat them until they were the consistency her mother used to tell her was just right for perfect scrambled eggs.

Somewhere between mixing the eggs and the smells of cooking bacon and baking biscuits, Caryn had a startling revelation. She had lost touch with reality—day-to-day, down-to-earth living. She had lost all personal contact with the very things she sang about in her songs—the simplicity of life and the satisfaction of love.

That realization frightened her even more than the men with the guns.

Life on the road was fast-paced and stressful. She was in one city in one state today and another city in another state, hundreds of miles away, tomorrow. For the first time, Caryn realized it had been that way for too long.

She felt suddenly remorseful with the realization that the one thing she sought more than anything beside her success had evaded her: Simplicity. A pure and simple life with time to savor the aroma of flowers and baking biscuits and the sight of a tranquil sunrise over the eastern horizon. But the demands imposed on her by the very nature of her occupation had taken all that away. She lived inside some magical fantasy bubble where there was always someone to do everything for her. The cost of success in her business was staggering. And the nights, the nights she used to spend thinking and dreaming in Georgia— where had they gone? Would they ever return, or had the glitter of her success erased that simple pleasure from her life forever? She wondered more than anything, as she stirred the eggs in the frying pan, if there would be a tomorrow. Would there be another chance to take advantage of everything that had slipped away before she even knew it? More importantly, how long was forever? Would it all end—the fame, the dream, the fantasy—would it end right here in the heartland of America on a humble Nebraska farm?

The very thought scared the hell out of her.

This was her third day of captivity, and she still wasn't sure what the people with the guns wanted. There had been no real explanation of their intent. Caryn would have been happy to pay the ransom demanded in her previous tape recording and end the ordeal. Deep inside, she knew it wasn't going to be that simple. There was much more. Right now, she didn't know what it was or why.

The only consolation she felt was within herself, retrieved from the depths of her inner strength. Caryn Collins, the woman, was a survivor. She knew that fact was unquestionable. Beneath the facade of her public image was a woman carved from raw determination, who had learned how to take the lumps and bumps, and sail on when times got hard. Right now, with a strange man holding a shotgun and watching every move she made, times were *very hard*.

The man who watched her didn't come across as the hard-core kind. His name even sounded subtle—Richie Halloway. Something about him bugged the hell out of her. The name . . . she would have sworn she had heard it before. Somewhere. But right now, Richie wasn't talking. His tape, the one she made for him last night, said a lot without saying anything. What did he want . . . *really*? Caryn decided to try to strike up a conversation while she and Marilee put the finishing touches on a breakfast for twenty-four people.

Caryn emptied the eggs from the frying pan into a large bowl. Then she turned to Halloway. "Do you mind if I call you Richie?"

Halloway looked surprised as if the words had caught him off-guard. "Yeah?"

"You must be starving. Would you like a little sample of the eggs and bacon before we start serving them to everyone else?"

Halloway hesitated. He wondered what Collins's ploy was. "Why would I want to do that?"

"You're the one in charge around here, aren't you?"

Halloway stiffened. "That's right. So?"

Caryn forced a smile. "So don't you deserve a few perks?"

"Perks?"

"Something special."

"Yeah, sure. I'll take some. This better not be a trick. I mean, why are you bein' nice to me?"

Caryn forced the smile again, trying to make it appear genuine. "Because I don't think you're like the others. I can see it in your eyes. You're different. Very different." She took a plate from the cabinet and filled it with eggs and bacon. Then she found a fork and laid it on the plate. "This isn't very formal, but it's the best I can do under the circumstances. Hope you enjoy it."

Halloway moved forward. He held the shotgun in one hand and took the plate with his other. He stepped back against the wall near the door. "Looks good. Just smellin' all this stuff in here makes me hungry."

Marilee watched Caryn and Halloway. She turned back to the oven and removed the biscuits. "You want a hot buttered biscuit to go with that?"

Halloway mellowed for just a moment, let his guard down. "Sure, why not?"

Marilee buttered a biscuit and handed it to Halloway. She immediately went back to the pan she had taken from the oven and removed the other biscuits from it.

Richie didn't waste time. He ate the eggs, bacon, and biscuit with a fury. But even while he ate, he kept one eye on the two women.

Caryn watched his every move. "Richie, we'll need some help getting all of this food to the others. Would it be all right to get one of the other girls to help?"

Halloway nodded as he devoured his breakfast. He reached around and opened the kitchen door. "Hey, Cliff. Come in here a minute."

Almost before the words stopped, Cliff Scott stood in the doorway. "Yeah, Rich?"

"Hey, man. Go get one of the other girls to come help get this food out. Let's get everybody fed so we can get on with things."

"Sure, Rich. Damn, man, this smells like *real* food. It's the first time I've smelled anything this good in years. I'll be back in a minute." Scott left and walked down the hallway to the large room where the other captives were held.

Caryn Collins had watched the scenario closely. In less than a minute, Scott reappeared with Dena Mullins, another of Caryn's backup singers. The three women prepared paper plates that had been salvaged from the tour buses. They readied the food and moved it to a large table in the dining room next to the kitchen.

Caryn looked at Halloway and forced one more smile. "Richie, we're ready for the others. Can they eat in here?"

Halloway wasn't sure what to say. He fumbled for words. "Uh, well . . . I don't know. Naw, take the plates into the other room. That'll be better."

"Okay, whatever you say." Caryn reached to the counter behind her when she was sure Halloway wasn't looking. She wrapped her hands around a small kitchen knife and held it firmly behind her back. She looked hard at Halloway, and then her lips parted in a broad smile. "We're ready, Richie."

Roy O'Connall had driven through the night. The highways had been mostly barren except for eighteen-wheelers and an occasional police car. As usual, he had disregarded posted speed limits; the speed limit was best selected by the individual and his capabilities. The Corvette ZR-1 devoured the blacktop and delivered him into Nebraska at breakneck speed. The radar detector clipped to the sun visor chirped only three times after he left St. Louis. Each time, he slowed just long enough to get past the source of the alert. When the threat was behind him, he resumed speeding.

O'Connall saw the exit signs for North Platte. He slowed the Vette, got into the right lane of Interstate 80, and took the first exit he came to, looking for a place to eat. He found a restaurant and drove into the parking lot. When he left the Vette and started inside, he spotted a newspaper rack. After fumbling through his pockets for the correct change, he inserted the coins into the slot and retrieved a newspaper.

O'Connall glanced at the front-page headlines, then found a seat. He ordered breakfast, folded the newspaper open on the table in front of him, and read the headline article with acute interest. Escapees. Murders. No trace. It all caused his mind to wander. Despite the fatigue of driving all night, his brain clicked off the possible associations. He wondered, could it be linked? After all, Caryn Collins had disappeared two days after the escape occured. He searched the newspaper for any tidbit that might mention Collins or her disappearance. There was nothing. But still Roy O'Connall wondered, and another possibility materialized on an ever-increasing list of possibilities.

The waitress returned with his order. O'Connall was finished in minutes. He paid his check, folded the newspaper under his arm, and left the restaurant.

Roy spotted a phone-from-the-car paystation, across the parking lot. He hopped in the Vette, drove to it, and placed a collect call to Shannon.

Shannon's secretary answered on the third ring in her usual efficient manner. She accepted the charges without question, and that told Roy this case must be very important to Shannon because the young girl usually questioned Roy's intent.

It took less than a minute for Shannon to come on the line. "Good morning, Roy."

Roy knew something was amiss. Shannon was never this pleasant when he spoke to him. "Hello, brother. Anything new and exciting that I should know about?"

"Yes, as a matter of fact, there is something that may be a possibility for you. Two days before Caryn Collins disappeared, there was a large prison break at the Nebraska State Penitentiary. Four guards were murdered, and four inmates escaped. All of 'em hard-time lifers."

"I read that much in the newspaper over breakfast. You know something the reporters didn't want to talk about?"

The comment struck Shannon as odd since he had seen nothing in the St. Louis newspaper. "Where are you?"

"North Platte, Nebraska."

"Why North Platte?" Shannon asked.

"That's where Caryn Collins played her last date before she disappeared. At least that's what your information said. By the way, has the press gotten wind of her disappearing act?"

"We don't believe it's an act, first off. Second, the answer is no. We're trying to keep a lid on it."

Roy hesitated. "Well, how long do you think you can do that before some nosy reporter gets suspicious?"

"As long as it takes."

Roy mumbled something unintelligible. He paused. "What's this 'we' shit you keep bringing up?"

"I'm afraid I don't understand."

"Bullshit. What is it that you're not telling me?"

"What?"

"Come on, counselor. Cut this misunderstanding shit and answer my question. You're hiding something. I want to know what it is."

"Roy, you're too suspicious. Maybe you need a vacation when this is over."

"Yeah, well, if you're buying, then maybe I do. If

you're not, then I don't need one. What's the score on this case? You're mighty interested in a couple of tour buses for some reason. What gives?"

"Like I told you, it's not the buses. They're the focus. We want Caryn Collins and her entourage. We want to know how they managed to completely vanish from the face of the earth. Find her."

"Come on, Shannon, you're jerking me around on something. Spill it."

"Really, Roy, there is nothing to spill. I've given you all the information I have on this. Honestly."

"Shannon, you're a lawyer. You've never been honest a day in your life. Beside that, you don't lie any better now than you did when we were kids. Let's have it. Explain this 'we' shit. And make me believe it this time."

"My client and I. That's 'we.' There is nothing else I can tell you."

"Asshole! Why don't you just say it? There's nothing else you'll tell me. You could, but you won't."

"Okay, have it your way. Believe whatever you'd like. If I get anything else, I'll be in touch. How can I reach you?"

Roy was pissed. "You can't. I'll call you from time to time."

"But what if I get further information and I need to—"

Roy interrupted. "Fret not, brother dear. I'll stay in touch."

"Now who's being the asshole?"

"You are!" Roy slammed the telephone receiver down, then hit the coin box with his fist. He heard the tinkle of change falling into the coin return and retrieved his change. He looked in his rearview mirror and smiled. "Ah, Roy, you did good. You made a quarter on this one. Not bad." He stuck the change in his pocket and turned the ignition key.

O'Connall reached for the newspaper on the passenger's seat. He opened the front page and tore out photographs of the four escapees. That done, he folded the photos and tucked them in his shirtpocket for future reference. His hand settled on the gearshift lever and dropped the selector into *drive*. Tires screamed when he started across the lot. Halfway across, O'Connall slammed on the brakes. He dropped the gearshift into *reverse* and backed up to the pay phone again. His right hand flipped through a black looseleaf telephone book and stopped on the *F*s. He scanned down the names with the tip of his finger until he found Jimmy Franklin.

Another coin hit the pay phone slot, and O'Connall dialed. Finally a voice answered and accepted the collect call. "Hey, Jimmy. Long time no see. What's been happening?"

The disgruntled voice answered. "Whatta you need this time, Roy? A hooker? Fake ID? What?"

"Jimmy, Jimmy. Such an attitude. Is that any way to greet a lifelong friend?"

"What is it, Roy? This is costin' me bucks."

"Okay, I need you to run something through Quality Facts. Can you handle it?"

"Hey, that's heavy. Them people got the goods on everybody for everything. It'll cost you."

"Doesn't it always? Okay, I want to know what kind of life insurance a woman by the name of Caryn Collins has on her head."

Jimmy breathed deeply, then sighed. "Okay. Caryn Collins. Could this be the country singer by the same name?"

"That make a difference?"

"Only in the price of the info. What's your interest in Collins?"

"I'm nosy. I was thinkin' about askin' her out on a date, and I want to be sure she's properly insured before she gets in the Vette."

"Yeah, shit. How soon do you need it, and where do I reach you?"

"I need it as fast as you can get it, and I'll have to call you. I'm in Nebraska. I'll be hard to reach."

"Nebraska? Shit, Roy. Do you know how much this phone call is gonna cost? Huh? Do you?"

"I'll pay you back. I promise."

"Right. You ain't finished payin' for all the other times yet. By the way, what about that hundred you owe me from a coupla weeks back?"

"Soon as I finish this case, I promise you'll get your money. Say, this has got to be costin' a bundle. I'll call you back in a couple of hours. Thanks, Jimmy. Bye." O'Connall slammed the receiver down before Franklin had a chance to answer. He hit the coin box with his fist again. Nothing happened. "How 'bout that? Some days you do, some days you don't."

———

Richie Halloway and Cliff Scott watched while the three women cleaned the kitchen. Everyone had devoured the meal as if it were their last. Each captive knew it might well be just that—his last.

Halloway leaned back against the wall beside the kitchen door. "Cliff, I want you to go into town this morning. We need supplies. Let's make a shopping list for whatever we might need for the next few days. Take the van and get everything. Don't go dogshit-wild when you get there. You're gonna have to lay low. I figure by now they've uncovered the fact that Amy was in the escape with us. If they have, the cops will be looking for both of you, so you gotta be cool."

Scott shrugged. "So we run into any nosy cops, we'll waste 'em. No big deal."

Halloway shot back. "No big deal, my ass. That's just what we *don't* need. Anything you do to attract attention will give the pigs an indication of where we are. Right now, I figure they're chasin' their asses because they got no idea which way we went. I wanna keep it that way. No screwups."

"Yeah, you're right. We'll be cool."

"When you get into town, I want you to buy from several places. Don't get everything in the same spot. Move around. If you make too big a purchase in one place, that'll arouse attention."

Scott agreed. "Okay. You know what you want?"

"You need to find a small air compressor, a paint gun, and some automotive paint. Talk to Ray. He's spent a lot of time in the paint shop at the joint. He'll know exactly what to buy."

"I don't understand. What are you gonna do with a spray painter?"

"Paint our ticket out of the country."

"What?"

"Those two tractor-trailers out there . . . they're our

way out once we get what we came for. We can't drive 'em the way they are. Every cop in the country will be lookin' for 'em. We can paint the mothers and change 'em around. That way, nobody could possibly recognize 'em."

Scott smiled. "I like it. You're smart, Richie. Real smart."

"Yeah. Don't forget to buy some beer. Make mine Coors—and whatever you guys want. We need a little celebration when we get ready to leave."

"Now you're talkin'. I ain't had a beer since I can't remember when."

"Don't start early. Don't even think about drinkin' while you're in town. It's much too risky."

"Where we gonna go when we get what we're after, Richie?"

"I'm not sure just yet. We gotta get out of the country, that's for sure. We're closer to Canada than we are to Mexico. Problem is, Canada will extradite if we get caught up there. Mexico won't. My gut says we need to make our way to Mexico. We get the trucks painted, and we can drive right across the border. Nobody will ever know the difference."

"Yeah, we go to Mexico, and we can go on into Central America or even South America. Who would know? Yeah."

"Get Amy in here. Let's get this show on the road."

"What are we gonna do with all these people?"

Halloway stroked the barrel of the Remington 870 shotgun affectionately with his hand. "That's up to them and how they handle my demands. They don't cooperate, we'll kill every damned one of 'em. Don't make me no difference."

CHAPTER SIX

The highway warriors rolled the customized Leeco over-road rig nonstop from Dallas to Nebraska. They decided to take turns driving while the other one slept. But for the first few hours on the road, both men studied the fax information transmitted to them by Brittin Crain at FBI headquarters in Washington. All four escapees were quickly climbing the popularity ladder in the Justice Department. Brittin had expressed expectations that the four would make the Ten Most Wanted list within hours. After all, escapees, especially violent murderers from a maximum-security facility, were not the kind of citizens society needed running around without restraints.

The warriors evaluated the possibilities and the consensus was that the coincidence was too great. Four hard-core types escape from a maximum-security facility, and two days later a celebrity superstar who just happens to be performing in the same general region vanishes without a trace. Fate or coincidence, a superficial case was certainly building.

Brittin Crain had agreed to poll the FBI agents assigned to the escape case. Marc knew Crain would dip into the information well until he came out with something concrete, one way or another.

Until there was word from Crain, the highway warriors decided to pursue whatever leads they could develop. If they could find one significant trace to connect the two disappearances, the stage would be set for a solution. Marc and Carl agreed that the first piece to the mysterious puzzle was probably near the point of Caryn Collins's final departure, North Platte. And that's where they were headed.

The second option led to even more possibilities. If the escape and the disappearance of Caryn Collins and her entourage were not related, then there were two cases that deserved the attention of the two roving cures for criminal disease. Both warriors hoped Brittin Crain could dispel one or the other possibility.

The FBI had not yet taken an official interest in Caryn Collins's mysterious vanishing act, probably because the people from her organization had requested that a lid be kept on the situation to avert the possibility of bad publicity. Shannon O'Connall had made that quite clear when Marc spoke with him by telephone. Something was out of place, and Marc wasn't quite sure what it was. It seemed strange that a celebrity wouldn't take advantage of any opportunity for press. Unless, of course, there was something someone was trying to hide.

And so the web grew more tangled. Marc hoped that by the time he and Carl reached North Platte, Brittin would offer something of value. Any information that narrowed the field would be welcome. But right now, there was little of substance to pursue.

One thing Marc was sure of. Somewhere in the United States the malignancy of four convicted killers grew. The putrid rot of decayed minds could potentially spread its infection with every day the four dirtbags remained outside either prison walls or a grave. And like a rampant and lethal virus, the infection possessed the ability to terminate innocent lives indiscriminantly. The President of the United States had decided that the criminal virus had to be exterminated with cleansing heavy firepower.

Marc and Carl spotted the exit signs for North Platte at the same time. Carl slowed the rig. "This one okay?"

"Sure. Let's grab a bite to eat before we get in too deep. What say?"

"Okay by me." Carl turned the rig onto the exit ramp. He reached the stop sign at the end of the ramp, looked both directions, and turned onto the two-lane highway toward a restaurant.

Marc yelled, "Look out!"

Carl slammed on the brakes as a fire-engine-red Corvette zoomed past the front bumper of the over-road rig. Carl stopped the rig within inches of the sports car. "Crazy son of a bitch! Tell me he can't see something as big as an eighteen-wheeler."

"Dumb asses are everywhere. I thought you had him there for a second."

"So did I. Where'd that idiot come from?"

"The parking lot at the restuarant. He was driving like a maniac."

Carl put the rig into low gear and started it moving again. "This rig would have made little slivers of that fiberglass ride if we'd hit that idiot."

"We could certainly live without that. Too many questions."

"Let's eat." Carl turned into the huge parking lot and shut the rig down.

Marc and Carl dismounted and walked across the parking area to the restaurant. Behind them, an automobile engine roared, and tires screamed as rubber clawed into blacktop. Marc and Carl turned, each instinctively reaching for the weapon concealed beneath his shirt. They had their hands on Smith & Wesson 5906s when the red Corvette screeched to a stop.

A man with red hair and a flaring temper to match jumped from the car the instant it stopped. "Hey, you! Where'd you learn to drive?"

Carl smiled a broad sarcastic smile. "You couldn't be talkin' to me, could you, boy?"

Roy O'Connall was furious. "Yeah, peckerwood, I'm talkin' to you. That's a fifty-thousand-dollar car you almost creamed."

Marc chuckled beneath his breath. He was thinking, So what's the big deal with a fifty-thousand-dollar car when you're driving a sixteen-million-dollar over-road rig custom built by presidential order? "You're the one drivin' like a bat out of hell," said Marc. "Sounds to me like you got more mouth than brains. Why don't you take that red piece of shit and pack it while you still can?"

O'Connall ignored the verbal barrage. "Who are you, smartmouth?"

"I'm the guy that's gonna sweep this parkin' lot with your butt if you don't get in that car and go on about your business."

O'Connall shot back. "I'm *scared*, man. Watch me tremble." He walked from beside the Vette toward Lee and Browne. "What's LFL stand for? Little Fat Ladies? That's about how tough you are, like a little fat lady." O'Connall kept walking.

Marc slid the Smith from its holster slowly, but he kept it out of sight. "Leeco Freight Lines, shitface. You want to complain, headquarters is in Dallas. In the interest of your well-being, I suggest you mount up in that hot machine of yours and make a rapid departure."

O'Connall slowed, but he didn't stop. "And what if I don't?"

Marc's face turned stone hard. He nodded toward Carl and spoke with ice in his voice. "Then me and him and the boys from Massachusetts are gonna rearrange your bad attitude."

"What boys from Massachusetts?"

Marc came out with the 9-mm automatic and leveled it at O'Connall's face. "Two of my best friends—Smith & Wesson."

O'Connall froze. His face flushed red, and for a moment it almost matched the color of his hair. "You and your friends are very convincing. My mistake. Until the next time..." He turned quickly and walked to the Vette. Without hesitation, he jumped in, slammed the gearshift into drive, and spun from the parking lot.

"Strange fellow," Carl said. "You think he was crazy enough to try and take both of us?"

Marc tucked the automatic beneath his shirt. "Not likely. Something tells me that guy was crazy like the proverbial fox. I just wonder what he was up to."

Carl was puzzled. "What do you mean?"

"That look. Especially his eyes. He searched us with his eyes, and then he picked us apart. He sized us up individually. And the way he talked. He was feeling us out for something. The argument was a facade. He knew we had guns. I could read it on his face. I've got a hunch we're going to see that man again. And probably sooner than we think."

———

Roy O'Connall had instantly recognized something very different about the two men from the Leeco rig. He was sure they were something other than day-to-day truck drivers. It showed in their faces, their eyes. And the tough-looking white guy with the gun: definitely not a normal truck driver.

The initial encounter at the intersection had been a coincidence. Roy realized he was driving like a maniac, but his mind was somewhere else. Had it not been for a glimpse of the small print on the bottom of the driver's door of the rig, he would have gone on his way without further concern. When he saw Leeco on the door, a little bell sounded an alarm in his head. He had studied the file of information Shannon had given him on the Caryn Collins case. One note of interest to him was the fact that Collins leased all her transportation. The buses were leased from Interstate Leasing, and the eighteen-wheelers used to carry her support equipment were leased from none other than Leeco Freight Lines.

It struck Roy that just maybe someone else was in on the hunt for Caryn Collins beside himself. And that thought bothered him. He figured there was only one way to find out. And that's just what he'd done. Once he had shot past the Leeco rig, the mental alarms and his natural curiosity had caused him to turn around and pursue the eighteen-wheeler. Now he was glad he had. Whether the drivers of that truck were straight or not, O'Connall had their number. He had seen their faces, and he wasn't likely to forget them because Roy O'Connall never forgot a face—especially when he had to look over the barrel of a gun to see it.

Roy mentally listed the white guy and the big black guy in the red Leeco tractor on the top ten of his ongoing shitlist. And when he did that, he decided that if and when there was another chance meeting with the two guys, the tables would most definitely be turned. Next time, he'd give them an introductory boxing lesson before they had time to reach for their hidden automatics.

After ten minutes of chastising himself, O'Connall decided he'd better get back to the real reason he had driven all night: Caryn Collins and the missing buses.

The fact that the trail to Collins cooled with every passing minute disturbed O'Connall. For several years, he had conducted many investigations, most for trucking companies or their insurers. The missing-entertainer business was a little out of his line. But Shannon had used a persistent and very convincing brotherly method to insure that Roy took the case. Roy reasoned that an investigation was an investigation, whether it was trucks or buses or missing entertainers. He had worked for Interstate Leasing in the past, but only on cases where trucks or their cargoes managed to vanish. And the top dogs in that company were usually more than just a mild pain in the ass. They were hard hitters, guys who wanted only one thing—results. They could care less about the method or the cost as long as the job got done efficiently.

The prevailing attitude of the management at Interstate Leasing was the main reason Roy ended up working on their toughest cases. Roy O'Connall got the job done, and he didn't concern himself with little details like the hows and the whys. Roy O'Connall's bottom line was successful efficiency. Nothing was barred from the O'Connall bag of dirty tricks, and if that meant treading less than gently on rules or laws, then too bad. He had learned his lessons long ago. The fundamental difference between success and failure in virtually any undertaking was simply persistence. And if Roy had one thing in the world going for him, it was persistence.

O'Connall turned the ZR-1 Corvette into the parking spot reserved for the comptroller at the North Platte Civic Center. He shut the rumbling engine off and went inside the giant entertainment facility. He glanced at his wristwatch and realized he was fifteen minutes early for his meeting with the director of the center.

Roy opened the office door and walked inside without knocking. A receptionist's desk was vacant. He looked around the front of the office and neither saw nor heard anyone. A cup of hot coffee sat on the receptionist's desk, but other than that, there were no signs of life.

"Hello," Roy said. "Anybody here?"

No answer.

"Hello, Mr. Roberts. Anybody. Hello."

Still no answer.

Roy walked back to a sofa in front of the desk and sat down. He picked up a magazine and thumbed through it. As he flipped the pages, he glanced at them but didn't really see anything.

Then he heard it. A moan. He heard it again, and this time he was sure: a whining sound like someone in pain.

O'Connall pitched the magazine back to the table. He was off the sofa and halfway down a hallway behind the receptionist's desk when he heard it again. This time it was behind him. He spun around. An office door. O'Connall stood beside the door with his right ear against the wall. He listened. He heard it again from inside the office. It was weaker this time.

O'Connall took a deep breath, held it, and waited. There was no other sound coming from the closed office, no indication of movement. He reached into the small of his back and wrapped his hand around the butt of his Colt Python .357 Magnum revolver. He eased the revolver from its holster and held it at arm's length against his leg. Roy pressed his ear harder against the wall, listening for anything that would tell him the source of the moan.

Nothing.

Roy moved his hand on the revolver grip, almost fondling it. He heard the moan again. Weaker this time and pain-filled. He reached to the door knob, twisted it gently. Locked. He stepped away from the wall and took mental aim. He thrust forward with all his weight shifted to his right foot. His foot struck the door just left of the knob. The impact caused the door to burst open then slam into the wall directly behind it. O'Connall was in a low crouch, the revolver firmly in his extended right hand. He rolled into the office with his index finger squeezing the trigger and his eyes searching for a deserving target.

He saw the source of the moan. She was there beside him—a woman who looked to be in her midtwenties lay sprawled on the floor. She had shoulder-length brown hair, part of which was matted in blood. Her eyes were rolled back in her head, and she tried to speak. Beside her, a large pool of blood formed on the floor. Her eyes focused on O'Connall and the gun in his hand. Her pain-filled face grimaced with fear.

O'Connall froze.

The woman spoke, her words etched with pain. "Please, no more. God, no, please don't hurt me anymore. Please!"

O'Connall realized the woman was focusing on the gun. He quickly tucked it into his waistband. "I'm not going to hurt you. Can you hear me?"

The woman nodded her head slightly.

"Okay, just lie still. I'll call for an ambulance. Just don't move. You'll be okay. Do you understand me?"

The woman nodded again.

O'Connall stepped over the woman and reached for a telephone on a desk three feet away. He picked up the receiver. "Operator, this is an emergency. I need the police and an ambulance at the North Platte Civic Center office. A young woman has been shot. She is semiconscious, bleeding heavily. Hurry!"

Roy slammed the receiver back into its cradle and turned around. That's when he saw a man on the floor behind the desk. O'Connall jumped over the desk for a better look. Most of the guy's chest was a massive open wound, and a single bloody circle dotted his forehead. There was no visible respiration, and his skin was turning blue-black. Roy reached to the man's neck and checked the carotid artery for a pulse. There was none.

Roy ran back to the woman. She was going in and out of consciousness. She had stopped moaning, her eyes locked in a gaze that seemed to see nothing. "Lady, listen to me. You'll be okay. Help is on the way. Can you tell me what happened here? Who did this?"

The woman didn't respond.

Roy reached into his hip pocket and came out with a handkerchief. He pressed it against the wound. "Lady, please, listen to me. Don't go to sleep. Please. Try to talk to me. Can you do that?"

The woman's weakening voice mumbled. "I'll try."

"Who did this?"

The woman strained to get the words out. "Man . . . and girl . . . van. Mr. Roberts . . . knew him. Caryn . . . Collins. Man . . . in van came back to . . . to kill . . . Mr. Roberts. No witnesses . . . prisoner . . ." The woman struggled for breath.

"A man and a girl in a van. Am I right?"

The woman managed a nod.

"Mr. Roberts knew him. Right?"

Another nod.

"The man in the van took Caryn Collins. He was with Caryn Collins. Which one?"

"Kid . . . napped her. Man in . . . van. Shot us.

"What color van? Can you tell me?"

"Blue. Dark . . . blue. T . . . V. Prisoner."

"A man in a dark blue van. Is the man who shot you one of the prisoners who escaped?"

The woman answered with a burst of breath. "Yes."

"Okay. Please hang on. Let me try to get all of this right. Now listen, help is coming. You'll be all right. A man and a girl in a dark blue van. The man is one of the escapees. He kidnapped Caryn Collins and came back to kill Mr. Roberts. Did I miss anything?"

The woman shook her head to indicate no.

"Did Mr. Roberts see the man kidnap Collins? Was Mr. Roberts there?"

The woman was struggling to get the words out. "Saw man . . . and van. Got on . . . bus. Mr. Roberts . . . he remem . . . bered man. Shot . . . us. Ohhh!"

The woman wrenched with pain. Her eyes closed, and she let out an agonizing moan that seemed never to end.

O'Connall took a deep breath and looked away. "Shit!" He looked back at the woman. "Lady, please, I know it hurts, but can you tell me one more thing? How long ago did this happen? Can you remember?"

The woman looked into O'Connall's eyes. "Not . . . long."

Roy ran his fingers through the front of the woman's hair. "Listen to me, honey. You're gonna be okay. The ambulance will be here any second. Hang on. I know you want to go to sleep. Don't. Stay awake. Talk to me.

Anything. Just don't go to sleep. You're hurt, but it isn't that bad. Really. Talk to me."

O'Connall was lying. There was little doubt the woman was mortally wounded. From the size of the hole in her chest, he was surprised she was still alive, much less conscious. He knew it was only a matter of time before the darkness of death overtook her.

"Why? I hurt. I didn't know that man . . . Mr. Roberts . . . did. He killed . . . me." A burst of breath came from the woman's lips. Her head sank back, then to one side.

O'Connall checked her neck for a pulse. She was still alive, barely. Roy looked around the office quickly. He pulled his shirttail out and wiped the telephone clean. He went to the door and wiped the knob clean. He realized there was nothing more he could do here. And there was one thing for sure: his meeting with Roberts would never happen. The man lay dead behind the desk.

Roy decided to haul ass before the paramedics and police arrived. Prudence before valor. And now a lukewarm case had suddenly turned scalding hot. There was no reason for the wounded woman to lie. People who thought they were dying didn't usually.

O'Connall worked his way back to the hallway he had walked through to enter the facility. He found another way out and got within sight of the Vette. He heard the sirens screaming in the distance. It was time to get away from Dodge.

He ran for the Vette, fumbling for his keys with one hand and securing the revolver with the other. He unlocked the door and started the engine. As he moved from the parking space, he caught a glimpse of a dark blue van speeding from the other side of the huge parking lot. O'Connall dropped the gearshift into *drive* and floored the accelerator. Tires squealed and burning rubber adhered to the pavement as the van disappeared behind the building.

CHAPTER SEVEN

Ray Hartley felt good for the first time in years.

Maybe it was freedom. Maybe the sweet taste of final revenge. He didn't know which, and he really didn't care. All he knew was, at last he had the opportunity he had dreamed of, had lain awake nights picturing over and over in his mind. He could finally finish what he had started nine years earlier. And he owed it all to Richie Halloway. Had it not been for Richie's burning desire to escape and take his own revenge, Hartley realized, he would probably have spent the remainder of his life behind prison walls.

Escape from a maximum-security prison was no easy task. Although the plan had worked flawlessly, it had not been without great preparation. And the key element had been Amy Markham. She had run the bread-delivery route every day for over a year. No one noticed, and no one knew her real intentions. The overlooked detail was the fact that Amy Markham had been born Amy Scott, sister of Cliff Scott. She had been married and divorced, but she retained her married name. With Amy driving a delivery truck into the prison compound and then out again, the escape had been merely a matter of timing and luck.

Hartley inserted the skeleton key into the two-way lock on the bedroom door. He twisted it and felt the bolt move free. His sawed-off shotgun was cradled in his arm when he opened the door. Hartley grinned when he saw Lilly Arthur's muscles tighten as she looked at him. "You ate good, old woman. I like that. I want you to be feisty when I take you out. You know, I should have made sure you were dead nine years ago. My mistake."

Lilly's eyes lit up in fear. The scars from that night of horror nine years ago had taken their toll. She was little more than a shell of a human being, a woman who lived her simple life and took the lumps accordingly. The fact that she had remained on the farm and managed somehow to keep it from failure was a miracle in itself. She fumbled for words, not sure whether to speak or just remain silent. "I wish you had killed me that night. You're a heathen, Ray Hartley. You're not a man, you're a sinful, devilish beast. When you killed my husband and my daughter, you killed me too. I only wish my body had died with my heart."

Hartley's face was hard, etched with the cold bitterness of a killer who placed no value on human life. "Me too, old woman. If you'd died, I wouldn't have spent the last nine years of my life in that hellhole. You were a lot tougher than I thought. You surprised me."

Lilly felt more courageous now. "Why don't you just go ahead an' kill me an' be done with it. That's what you're gonna do anyway. Put me out of my misery."

Hartley laughed. "Oh, no. That's too simple. I want you to feel some of the hell I felt for these nine years. I loved your daughter, and she loved me. She had my baby inside her, but you and your puritan values . . . you wouldn't let us have the life we wanted. I didn't want to kill her. It was an accident. I was gonna shoot the old man, and she stepped in front of me. I didn't even know she was pregnant until the trial 'cause you wouldn't let me see her. She loved me, you old bitch."

Lilly stared into Hartley's eyes. "She never loved you. She was a young girl blossomin' into a woman. She didn't know no better. She mistook the cravin' of her body for love and you, the lowlife you are, took advantage of that. You're a heartless, sinful heathen."

Hartley's face lit with rage. "You're a lyin' bitch. She *did* love me. You don't know what love *is*, old woman. Me and her loved each other."

"You'll burn in the pits of hell for what you've done, Ray Hartley. You'll reap the crops of your sinful seeds. Maybe I won't be there. But if I die before you, I'll walk the gold-paved pathways of heaven at the right hand of the Lord Jesus while you burn in hell."

Hartley's face was flushed with anger. Her jerked the shotgun to his shoulder and walked toward Lilly, shaking with rage. His body trembled; the barrel of the shotgun vibrated up and down.

"I'm gonna kill you, old woman. What you did to me was wrong. You think you're so holy and righteous. Bullshit. You're a lyin' old bitch. You're gonna die!" Hartley was screaming, his mind and his body out of control. He shoved the huge barrel of the twelve-gauge against the woman's nose and pushed the safety off. "You're gonna die!"

A smile split Lilly's face. She closed her eyes. Her voice mellowed and filled with tenderness. "I ain't afraid to die like you are, Ray Hartley. Go ahead, kill me. I'm ready to go home to Jesus. Please kill me an' send me home with my family an' sweet Jesus."

Hartley was stunned. "You're nuts, you dumb old bitch. You really *want* to die. You're insane." Hartley's finger trembled on the trigger as he eased it back. "Well, bitch, I'm gonna take pleasure in splatterin' your brains all over this room. Bye!"

Lilly was unmoved. She closed her eyes tightly and whispered a prayer. "The Lord *is* my shepherd, I shall not want. He maketh me to lie down in *green* pastures. He leadeth me beside the still waters for *his* name's sake. He restoreth my soul. My cup runneth *over*. Yea though I walk through the valley of the shadow of death, I will fear no evil . . . ."

———

Marc noticed the message light on the computer screen the instant he opened the door to the customized Leeco over-road rig. The message was brief and to the point: *Contact Brittin Crain immediately.*

Carl settled into the driver's seat. "The boy must have something hot. You gonna give him a call?"

Marc reached for the Icom microphone connected to the IC-V100 transceiver on the communications console. "Yeah, maybe he has some updated information for us. I'm proud of him and the job he's doin' in D.C. I never thought he could settle down that much."

"I hope he has something, 'cause right now we got a big goose egg for leads. Nothing adds up. The time we're wasting could be costing lives if this kidnapping thing is real. If it isn't, we could be chasin' those escapees. Way I see it, either way, we're wasting valuable time."

Marc nodded his head. "I couldn't agree more. I'm ready to get down to action and move on something." Marc punched the channel-select switch and stopped on channel twelve. "Barnburner, this is Pathfinder. Over."

Brittin's voice came across the speaker at almost the same instant Marc released the transmit switch on the microphone. "Pathfinder, this is Barnburner. Glad you got back to me so soon. The Bureau's bustin' its balls on this escape case. I've got some updates for you. Some of it is only ten minutes old. Are you ready to copy?"

Marc keyed the microphone. "Roger, Barnburner. I'm activating the recording system as we speak. We're ready on this end. Go ahead with your traffic."

"Roger. These escapees are hard-core types. All of 'em are lifers or multiple lifers. I have complete case histories now, and I'll fax those to you when I'm finished with the verbal information. Here's the latest. About twenty minutes ago, the manager of the North Platte Civic Center was killed. His secretary was critically wounded. She was conscious enough to tell the first officer on the scene that the man who killed the manager was one of the escapees. They notified the Bureau immediately. Here's the pisser: In the case histories, one of the escapees, from North Platte, killed a farmer and his daughter there nine years ago. A lost-love deal. Name of Ray Hartley. The dead girl's mother was seriously wounded but lived to testify against Hartley at his trial. He got two consecutive life sentences. The warden and some of the guards suspect Hartley is off on a course of retribution, and they're layin' odds Hartley is goin' after the old woman. You copy so far? Over."

Marc and Carl's attention focused on the Icom speaker. "Roger, Brittin. I copy. You've got our complete attention. Over."

"Roger. The special agent in charge from Omaha thinks he has made a link in the method of escape. A bread-delivery truck was found abandoned about twenty-five miles from the prison. From tire impressions, it appeared there was another vehicle waiting for the truck. If the tie-ins are correct, then the driver of the bread truck was in on the escape. She drove them right straight through the front gate of the facility. Nobody looked, nobody questioned. Over."

Marc looked puzzled. He keyed the microphone. "You said the driver was a woman. Does it look like she was a willing participant?"

Brittin's voice crackled through the speaker across the ComSat-D nationwide repeater system. "That's affirmative, Pathfinder. The driver hasn't been heard from since. Her name is Amy Markham. A fast background turned up an interesting fact about the young lady. She's Cliff Scott's sister. He's one of the escapees. Over."

Marc pressed the transmit switch. "My, my, you *are* full of surprises. What else? Over."

"Here's one you'll like. I think this provides the link you've been looking for. Richie Halloway was one of the escapees. He was serving three life sentences for hijacking a consignment load of firearms from an eighteen-wheeler at a rest area in central Nebraska. He killed the driver and two armed guards in a support van that followed the rig. Halloway is a bad boy. He kills for kicks. Now, here's your possible link. The word at the prison was that Halloway fancied himself a songwriter. He claims to have written a song that is the current record Caryn Collins has out. Problem is, Halloway's name doesn't show up anywhere on the record. The papers filed with the copyright office show Caryn Collins and some guy named Bernie Aldridge as the writers. Word in the joint was that Halloway went mad when he found out that the song was out and he had been cut out of it. They suspect he engineered the escape to take out Aldridge and Collins. A copy of Collins's fan-club newsletter was found in Halloway's cell. She had a performance scheduled in North Platte two days after the escape. My gut shot is that we have a solid link in Collins's disappearance and the prison escape. I think we got some bad boys who want to settle some conflicts. I'm bettin' on a trail of blood, and I think it started at the North Platte Civic Center. Over."

Marc absorbed all of Brittin's information. He didn't say anything for a moment. "Can you give us more information on the location of this farm where Hartley committed his murders? Over."

"I'll fax a map with as much information as we have at the moment. It may be a long shot, but the Bureau has more agents coming from Omaha to assist in checking out the farm. If the guesses are right and if these inhumans are there with Collins and company, there could be a real serious bloodbath. If you hustle, you might be able to get in before the Bureau does. If you can make verification, it might make the job a little easier. Over."

Marc pressed the button. "You guys are doing good work. You're a lifesaver. Maybe literally. Over."

"One more thing, Marc. Keep your eyes open for a dark blue Dodge van with Nebraska registration VKV-nine-four-seven. It's registered to Amy Markham, and it disappeared the same time she did. It was probably the vehicle used when the bread truck was abandoned. There's no doubt that these dirtbags will be heavily armed. Cover your asses, and don't take any chances. The boss wants them . . . well, do whatever is necessary, but don't get yourselves killed."

Richie Halloway heard the sound of the car coming into Lilly Arthur's long, winding driveway the very instant the gravel crunched under the tires. He ran to the front window, gently moved the curtains back, and looked out. "Holy shit! A cop. Oh, shit! Ray! Quick, get down here. There's a cop car comin'. Lionel!"

Hartley dropped the shotgun from Lilly Arthur's nose and ran to the door when he heard Halloway yell. He opened the door and glanced back at Lilly Arthur, who still sat with her eyes closed, mumbling Scripture. "You got a stay this time, bitch. But you're gonna die!" He entered the hallway outside the bedroom, shut the door, and locked it. In a few long strides, he was at the bottom of the steps in the living room. "Where's the pig?"

"There, comin' up the driveway. He's goin' real slow like he's checkin' the place out."

Lionel Lewis came from the room where the captured entourage was held. "Whatta we gonna do, Rich? We can't waste the mother. We do that, and every oinker for five hundred miles is gonna come in here shootin'. Whatta we do?"

Halloway's voice was shaking. "Let me think, man. I need to think."

Hartley wasn't quite as nervous, his fears turned into hatred. "Think, my ass. You shoulda done that before the cops got here. We got no time to think. We gotta do somethin', or the shit's gonna fly. Hell, Rich, I thought you had this planned out, man."

Halloway was rattled. "Yeah, yeah. I don't need none of your shit, Ray. Be cool. Run upstairs and get the old broad. When the cop comes to the door, we'll have her answer it. If she tips him off, we'll waste 'em both."

Hartley was already moving when he answered. "Okay, I'll get the old broad, but she's mine. You got that? She's mine. Nobody wastes the old bitch 'cept me."

Richie was in no position to argue. "Sure, Ray. You got her. Just get her ass down here before the cop gets to the door. Hurry!"

Lionel Lewis hoisted the submachine gun to his waist and flipped off the safety. "Whatta you want me to do, Rich?"

"Get back in there with Collins's people. Make sure they're all quiet. They can't see this cop car from where they are. Don't let 'em know what's goin' down. If anybody says anything or gives you any shit, cut his damned throat."

"Gotcha, my man." Lewis was moving down the hallway mumbling aloud. "I don't believe this shit, man. A cop. How the hell did a cop find us?"

Richie Halloway glanced over his shoulders at the sound of footsteps coming down the stairway. Ray Hartley stood directly behind Lilly Arthur. His shotgun touched the middle of her back as he nudged her forward. "Hurry it up, Ray. Get the old woman down here."

"We're comin', man. Be cool."

"Yeah, yeah, so is the cop. He's almost at the house. He drove out to the barns, but he didn't stop. I don't think he saw anything. He'll be on the front porch any second."

Hartley and Lilly Arthur stopped at the front door. The old woman, very frail and weak, stood with her chin almost touching her chest.

Halloway knew there was going to be trouble. "Look here, old woman. There's a cop out there. He's probably comin' to the door. When he does, you be real cool. You let him know we're in here, and I'll blow both of you through the front door. You hear me?"

Lilly nodded her head.

"Okay, you get rid of him. You screw up, and you're both dead."

Hartley interrupted. "Rich, the old woman wants to die. She don't care no more."

"Is that right, old woman?"

Lilly Arthur didn't answer.

"Okay, bitch. So you want to die. That's just fine. But I'll bet that cop ain't real anxious to go to the pearly gates. If you don't want him to die, you do just what we told you. Mess up, and I mean it, I'll kill both of you."

Hartley was angry now. "Hey, Rich, I told you the old bitch is mine. She's mine, man."

"Ray, shut up. I don't care who kills her. Get up the stairs. Wait at the top where the cop can't see you. If you hear something go bad, come get the old broad. I'll take care of the cop."

"Where you gonna be, Rich?"

"I'm goin' out the back and get at the side of the house where the cop can't see me. I can hear from there. When he stops the car, I'm goin' out the back. Listen to every word the old woman says. If she tips the pig, blow her away."

"I'd love to."

Richie looked out the window once more. The sheriff's car stopped in front of the house. For the first time, Richie could see clearly into the car. "Oh, shit! Shit!

There's two of 'em. Two damned cops, and one's going toward the back of the house!"

———

Dennis Goodman was standing near the window looking toward the fields behind the house when he saw the deputy sheriff walk by. At first Goodman was startled, but then he realized it was an opportunity that might never return. He remembered the 9-mm automatic in Mike Coble's toolbox. He and Coble had talked during breakfast and laid the tentative plan. It looked like this might be the distraction they were looking for.

Goodman eased over to Mike Coble. He whispered softly, "Cop just walked behind the house. This is our chance. You distract the little weasels, and I'll make a break for the rig. Maybe the cop will have a chance to help us before the shooting starts."

Lionel Lewis was at the end of his nerves. "You two back there, shut up. I mean it, don't say nothin'."

Coble felt lucky. "What are you gonna do, Lionel, shoot us? You might get some of us, but those cops outside are gonna come down on you like stink on shit. If we ain't beat you to death before they get to you, they'll just waste your black ass."

"Shut up, big man." Lionel reached to his hip and came out with a survival knife. He wielded the knife in his left hand. "I don't have to shoot your ass. I'll cut your damned tongue out if you don't keep quiet."

Coble kept moving toward Lewis. "I don't think so, Lionel. You see, you cut my tongue out, and all these pretty women are gonna start screamin', and the cops will come in shootin'. I think you're screwed, Lionel. I think your game is over."

Lewis was holding firm with the knife in one hand and the small submachine gun in the other. "Get back from me, honky. I'll cut you."

Coble kept moving. "Yeah, sure you will, Lionel. You're real tough with that gun and knife. I'll bet you're just a dark brown wimp when you're not loaded down with artillery. I'll bet you ain't shit." Coble was only a few feet away from Lewis now, watching the knife in Lewis's hand.

Lewis lunged with the sharp blade. Coble sidestepped and landed a left hook into the side of the black man's face. Lewis stumbled.

At precisely the same instant, Dennis Goodman grabbed a straight-backed chair and threw it through the window. Glass shattered and crashed to the floor inside and the ground outside. In a motion that made him look like he was gliding on air, Goodman leapt through the window and landed on the ground.

Lionel regained his balance and came around with the knife. The leading edge of the blade caught Mike Coble in the side and left a log cut. Coble screamed and came around with a right fist that connected with Lionel's jaw, grabbing the submachine gun from Lewis in the same motion. A sporadic burst of fire spit from the gun, and the scorching death pellets struck Lewis in the side. An involuntary reflex from the sudden pain brought Lewis's left arm around in a swinging arc, and the tip of the blade slashed through Mike Coble's throat. Both men fell to the floor amid screams from the hostages and splattering blood.

CHAPTER EIGHT

Roy O'Connall had steered the Corvette sideways onto the highway beside the civic center. He had cut hard left to straighten the sliding car, but it was broadsliding. He cut right, then left again until the Vette finally straightened. He slapped the accelerator to the floor and the mighty LT-4 380-horsepower engine roared.

O'Connall searched the road ahead for the blue Dodge van. Traffic was sparse, and he could see several blocks in front of him, but the van wasn't there.

Roy rode the streets for thirty minutes, searching side streets, parking lots, businesses, but there was no sign of the van. He watched police and medical response units descend upon the civic center. O'Connall mentally replayed the event that had taken place inside the center office. He knew that the good-citizen thing to do was to notify the local police of both his presence and the information the wounded girl had given him. That would point the legal fingers in the right direction of at least one of the escapees. He decided that being a good citizen and being a good investigator weren't always compatible. He decided to be a good investigator and keep his mouth shut. If the wounded girl regained consciousness, she could give the police the same information she had given him. If she didn't make it, then he was sorry for her. Either way, he figured he had a head start on the tentacles of the law. And it would look better for him if he captured the murderers rather than having the boys in blue do the job.

Roy understood that the odds of finding the blue van decreased with each passing minute. In any metropolitan area, finding one vehicle among many was like seaching for a single grain of black sand on a white beach. Without some indication of where the van was headed, there was little to rely on but luck. And Roy also knew that luck alone was seldom accommodating when it came to solving cases. Among the many vital things he had learned over the years was the fact that people who were successful at virtually anything most often made their own "luck" through diligent work and unending persistence. Right now, the question was how he could make Lady Luck smile upon him and put him on the scent of the killers.

A fleeting thought crossed his mind. What if the van he had seen leaving the civic center had nothing to do with the killing? What if he was searching for the wrong vehicle?

The thoughts made him very uncomfortable, so he decided to rid his mind of anything negative and concentrate on the positive. If the van was involved and it was occupied by the persons responsible for the death of the manager, and if one of the escapees was indeed involved, then he could find his backside squatting over a hornet's nest. But then and there O'Connall decided that if he encountered the van, he'd back off and give the occupants a chance to lead him into the den. From then on, he would just have to wing it.

Fifteen frustrating blocks from the civic center, O'Connall crossed an intersecting street where every other business looked like some kind of automotive supply. He shot casual glances right and left as he went through the intersection. As he reached the other side, he caught a glimpse of what appeared to be the back end of a dark blue van; the taillights were on. Roy quickly glanced into his rearview mirror. Three cars, one right on his bumper. He tapped his brakes, looked into the oncoming lane, and did an accelerated U-turn in the middle of the street. Horns honked and tires screeched as he stomped on the gas pedal. The Vette roared back into the intersection, and O'Connall cut hard right onto the street leading to the van. As soon as he was on the street, he realized what he had seen was gone. He slowed quickly and eased forward to where he thought he had seen the back end of the vehicle.

Nothing.

O'Connall slammed his fist into the passenger's seat of the Vette. "Damn! I know I'm not seeing things." He slowly continued forward, but there was still no sign of the van. He was in front of the store where he thought he had seen the vehicle. To his surprise, it wasn't an automotive supplier but a wholesale paint company. And that didn't make sense.

Roy mumbled to himself, "Shit! How many dark blue vans could there be in North Platte, Nebraska? I blew it." He reached another intersection just past the paint store. He slowed for a stop sign when he saw the dark blue van again. This time, the vehicle was three blocks ahead of him. O'Connall tapped the Vette's accelerator and spun out from the stop sign. He was gaining on the van when the driver signaled his intention to turn to another business. Roy slowed again, holding back so he wouldn't attract attention. He stopped across the street from the business and glanced at the sign above its doors: Air Equipment Corporation.

He waited.

The doors to the van popped open. A young woman—blond, slender build, and somewhere in her late twenties—stepped from the passenger's side of the van. She wore tight, faded jeans, a loose tank top, and jogging shoes. The woman stopped at the front of the van and looked toward the driver's side. A man, probably over six feet, with long brown hair and enough growth of beard that O'Connall could distinguish it from where he sat, stopped beside the woman. They glanced over the a slip of paper the woman held. After a few seconds of conversation that O'Connall couldn't understand, they entered Air Equipment.

Roy fumbled in his shirtpocket for the newspaper clipping he had torn out earlier in the day. He found it and then unfolded it on his leg. He looked at the pictures of the four escaped inmates, then glanced back at the doorway where the man and woman had disappeared. He couldn't say for sure, but it was possible . . . maybe Cliff

Scott, but the Cliff Scott in the picture had a full beard. There was one way he could find out.

O'Connall drove slowly across the street and parked beside the van. He jumped from the Vette and walked into Air Equipment.

Inside, the building was like almost every other wholesale distributing company Roy had ever seen. A single L-shaped counter occupied the front of the building. Behind it, rows of shelving that ran from the floor to the ceiling were filled with parts. In front of the counter, a row of worn stools in no particular order. The counter had a brown formica top and rough wooden sides. Besides the unassuming displays of various air-operated equipment, the most prominent thing in the front of the building was a sign that hung suspended from the ceiling: *Employees Only Permitted Behind Sales Counter.* That was just what Roy had hoped for, because to his left, seated on stools, sat the man and the woman from the van.

Roy looked around the room, then walked to the counter. He took a stool beside the woman and propped his elbows on the counter. The girl was looking toward the man on her other side. Roy wanted a good look at her. "Excuse me, miss. Aren't you Diane Morgan? I'm Dick, Dick Reynolds. You remember me, don't you?"

The woman turned around, shocked. At first there was a look of fear in her eyes but that soon faded into annoyance. She looked hard at O'Connall, her eyes locking with his. "You must be mistaken. I'm not Diane."

"Oh, gee, I'm terribly sorry. You just look so much like Diane Morgan. We went to school together. Haven't seen her in fifteen years or so. I didn't mean to offend you. I, uh, didn't catch your name."

The woman looked annoyed. "You didn't catch it because I didn't give it."

"Ah, okay. Look, really, I'm so sorry. You know anything about O-rings?"

The woman took a deep breath and sighed. "No, I don't. I'm just here with my friend. Anything else?"

Roy thought it strange that the man with the woman hadn't said anything when it was so obvious he was annoying her. "Uh, no. Again, I apologize. You really do look so much like Diane Morgan."

A salesman appeared behind the counter. "Who's next?"

"They are," Roy said and pointed toward the man and woman.

The salesman turned back to the man sitting beside the woman. "What can I get for you?"

"We're looking for a medium-capacity portable air compressor. Do you have one?"

The salesman nodded. "What do you plan on using it for?"

"A spray-paint gun."

"You gonna paint inside or outside?"

"Inside."

"Walls or a car? What type of service?"

"A car."

"Yeah, I think we'll have just what you need. It's three hundred and thirty-nine dollars plus tax for the hundred-and-ten-volt model. Will that work for you?"

"We'll take it."

The salesman disappeared behind the rows of shelves. Two or three minutes later he returned, carrying a large cardboard box. "Here we go. I'll get your ticket. Will this be cash or charge?"

"Cash."

The salesman looked at Roy. "Sir, I'll be right with you."

Roy smiled. "Uh, let me ask you a quick question. You got O-rings for a Scott airpack?" Roy expected a reaction from the man and woman, but none came.

"The breathing apparatus?"

"That's right."

"No, don't carry that kind of thing. Check with Staunton's Safety Equipment on West Eighteenth. They carry all of the safety-equipment lines. They'll have it."

"Okay, thanks. Sorry to interrupt."

Roy stood from the stool and went back to the Corvette. He took a hard look in the van as he passed by it. Beneath the edge of the driver's seat, a piece of dark wood protruded slightly, mostly covered by a towel. A gun stock perhaps? He unlocked his door and climbed in. The engine fired perfectly on the first tap of the starter, and he dropped the Vette into gear. He drove from the small parking lot and parked half a block down the street where his view of the van was clear. He slid the newspaper clipping from his shirtpocket one more time and analyzed it carefully. There was no doubt about it. The man in the store was Cliff Scott, sans the beard.

He waited, developing his plan. His right hand switched on the car radio, and the DJ speaking across the airwaves introduced the next record. It was a country tune, beautifully sung by Caryn Collins. As he listened, Roy wondered where the superstar was right now, or if she was still alive. Then he saw Cliff Scott and his female companion step through the door toward the van.

Marc drove the rig north on U.S. 83 out of North Platte. With the information furnished by Brittin Crain and the Justice Department, the highway warriors determined that little if anything could be gained by hanging around North Platte. In all likelihood, any evidence that might have existed would now be swept away by time. And right now, time was one thing Marc and Carl figured they couldn't afford to waste.

Brittin had agreed to have the FBI contact the Thomas County Sheriff in central Nebraska. Both Crain and Marc had decided it would be best to withhold as much information as possible from the sheriff when the request for a welfare check was made. Instead of causing unsubstantiated alarm for either the sheriff or Lilly Arthur, Crain suggested they simply inform the local lawman that Ray Hartley had escaped from prison and ask him to check on the elderly Arthur to be sure she was still in good health.

The regional office of the FBI in Omaha had agents en route to North Platte and the remote section of Thomas County that Lilly Arthur called home. It was a hunch best played to assure the safety of Mrs. Arthur.

Brittin Crain had learned to call the plays of the sick criminal mind over the years. Some of it was gut feeling, some pure fate or luck, and some simply good police work. Criminals hell-bent on retribution, whether in North Platte, Nebraska, or Dallas, Texas, usually behaved in a similar manner. Once a good cop had established behavioral patterns and committed them to memory, intelligent speculation became a daily tool.

After carefully analyzing the information Crain had received on Ray Hartley, his instincts told him where Hartley was going and what he planned to do when he got there. And if Hartley was still in the company of Halloway and the others, taking out a virtually defenseless old woman would be easier than snatching a bottle from a baby. After all, what did a guy like Ray Hartley have to lose? The farmboy-turned-dirtbag had already broken the most serious of society's rules. And with two consecutive life sentences and probably a death sentence for killing a guard during the escape, Ray Hartley was a man with everything to gain and nothing to lose. Killing Lilly Arthur would heal the wounds tormenting his sick mind and make his miserable life complete.

Marc had intensely studied the fax data transmitted to the over-road war machine. Among the four escapees, it was a toss-up between Ray Hartley and Richie Halloway as to which one seemed the less likely candidate for a life in prison. According to the background information that had become a permanent part of each man's case file, neither man had followed the normal course of events that led to a life of crime.

People like Ray Hartley who grew up in small rural communities didn't normally fall victim to the ravages of criminal infection like so many kids in the big cities. For Hartley, as best Marc could determine, it was simply a matter of love or desire over common sense. People just didn't go around in the heartland of America blowing other people away for the hell of it. Hartley's case read like so many other everyday American tragedies. Maybe there was simply a sequence of events that caused a normally respectable boy to turn into a cold-blooded killer. But once he made the turn, squeezed the trigger the first time, there was no turning back. Whether it was passion or a power play, taking another human life without *real* justification was legally, morally, and eternally wrong. The instant the first drop of innocent blood was intentionally spilled, Ray Hartley joined the ranks of dirtbag criminal scum. The transition from an innocent love-torn farmboy to hunted criminal filth took place in less than a heartbeat. And like the life that fled from his victim's bodies, innocence left Ray Hartley with the twitch of a finger on a trigger. And it could never, ever return.

Carl read more of the case histories on the escapees while Marc drove. Neither warrior spoke; their minds were consumed with thoughts of another war to be fought. The road from North Platte to Thedford was a great place to think. Marc's thoughts slipped back to Dallas and his father, Marcus Lee. He wondered how long a coma could last and how long the body of man in his sixties could be sustained without consciousness. He thought of his mother and uncle, themselves fatal statistics of rampant criminal scumbags. Marc knew that even he and Carl were victims of needless violence inflicted by diseased minds. He knew that his life, his family's life, would never be the same since the bloody, violent scythe of the grim reaper had swept through it. Nothing he or Carl or Brittin Crain or even the President of the United States could do would ever change the fact that his own family had been torn apart by dirtbags who preyed upon innocents.

And now, traveling a lonesome highway in middle America, Marc was on his own course of vengeance for the sake of undiluted justice. In America, lawlessness was a disease that knew no cultural or economic boundaries. It was colorblind and deaf. And while mankind had achieved vast technological expertise that grew by daily giant steps and constantly improved the quality of life for virtually every American, society, technology, and abundant education had failed to improve the very beings for which it was designed.

It was a sad state of affairs when citizens watched victims being raped on the streets and did nothing. And when witnesses to violence refused to come forth and do their moral duty by helping to rid the streets of criminals, then civilized society had failed. But it wasn't difficult to understand why the prevailing attitude of complacency and apathy ran as rampant as criminal behavior. When known perpetrators of criminal acts were set free by a system that represented *justice* simply because they could afford prominent and expensive attorneys, something was wrong. The system had failed the very people it was designed to protect and serve.

And that was the reason Marc and Carl were rolling across America's highways by request of the President of the United States: to return the country to a state where the rights of innocents were protected and defended and the perpetrators of violence and wrongdoing got just what they deserved—undiluted justice.

When the highway warriors delivered justice, there was no escape, no opportunity to perpetrate more violence against innocents. The very over-road rig in which he and Carl rode was designed to be a technologically advanced delivery system for swift and permanent justice. The President had committed sixteen million dollars of American taxpayers' money for the development and construction of the one-of-a-kind rig. And while that was a great deal of money by virtually any standard, it was negligible in comparison to the monetary waste that daily flowed through a criminal justice system that had failed its citizens.

Marc and Carl were not vigilantes. They were men charged with a duty to their country and their fellowman, tapped by the chief law enforcement officer in the United States, the President himself. They were the point men, the functionaries, of a project designed to restore law and order in a land smothered by lawlessness.

Right now, Caryn Collins was an innocent. And the indications were that she had fallen victim to the bacteria that Marc and Carl sought to eradicate. And there was Lilly Arthur—victim turned witness and probably victim again if the information Brittin Crain had was accurate. Somewhere outside Thedford, Nebraska, there was a very real possibility that the bacteria were out of control. And if the supposition proved fruitful, the cure for the disease was on the way. If necessary, the highway warriors would sanitize the land around them with cleansing fire and destroy this latest growth of criminal cancer.

Thanks to the highly advanced electronic technology

that filled the rig, Marc and Carl were able greatly to reduce their response time to the suspected location of this, the latest rape of innocents. They carried on board a system of data transfer and communications second to none in the free world. The rig was designed to be a "go anywhere, do anything" fighting system. And as yet, the technology had not failed.

Carl broke the silence. "The navaid says we should be near Thedford. You want me to pull up a topo map of the area on the screen?"

Marc cleared his throat. "Yeah, do that. Brittin's fax map had coordinates on it. When you get the topo, enter the coordinates, and let's see where we are in reference to the farm."

"Got it." Carl entered numerical strings until the proper map was displayed in full color on the computer screen. When he had the map, he opened the fax file and found the longitude and latitude of Lilly Arthur's farm. He entered the numbers. In seconds, a bright red line appeared on the screen ahead of a blinking blue dot. The dot represented the Leeco rig, and the red line charted the nearest specific geographic route to the farm. "There it is. All we got to do is keep the blue dot on the red line, and we're there."

Marc's voice was serious, concerned. "I hope that red line isn't drawn in innocent blood."

CHAPTER NINE

Dennis Goodman knew he was cut. He could feel the blood oozing from his legs and his shoulder. He felt the burning when the jagged edges of the glass ate into his flesh as he cleared the window. But that wasn't the burning he had expected. He had anticipated hot copper-sheathed lead to perforate his body before he could get his legs moving once he was on the ground. The loud bursts chattered behind him, but to his surprise, the searing pain never came. He knew he had made it when his shoes clawed into the ground and he ran all-out for the barn. He had decided that if the captors didn't get him in the first fifty feet, he was home free.

Goodman poured every ounce of strength into his legs and feet. He was a hundred feet from the house now and closing fast on the barn.

"Stop!"

The voice came from behind him, bitter cold and filled with authority.

Then it came again. "Stop!"

Goodman gave it everything he had. More energy came from a new burst of strength he didn't even know was there. His lungs burned from his struggle for more breath. And his shoulders, his legs, burning first from the wounds and then from the sudden burst of physical exertion. But even through the pain, his desire to survive overshadowed all else. Only a hundred feet remained between him and the safety of the barn. He could see it, feel the weapon in his hands, and see the bastards who had done this to the troupe lying dead before him.

The cold voice came again. "You son of a bitch, I said stop!"

Only seventy-five feet remained. Goodman could see the doors standing ajar, an easy entry.

The voice was irate now. "Stop, or I'll ream you a new asshole!"

Fifteen feet to go. Dennis Goodman glanced over his shoulder—he didn't know why but he did. He had no intention of stopping and destroying the only chance he and everyone else in Caryn Collins's group had of living to see tomorrow.

He felt the searing, excruciating pain in the same instant he saw the flash. And then he saw the man with the gun. The cop. The deputy sheriff was shooting at *him*.

Goodman screamed. "God, no! I'm one of the good guys." He fell to the ground, and he felt like the front end of the show bus had run over him. He screamed again. "Please, help us! We're kidnapped."

The roar of the deputy's revolver drowned out his words. Dirt flew near his head. Goodman scrambled, crawling, kicking, trying to get into the barn. Then a new pain. This one burned through his thigh like a red-hot poker and tumbled to a stop in his hip. He screamed as loudly as he could. His mind played tricks on him. It was impossible: he, Dennis Goodman, never-bother-anybody, mind-your-own-business Dennis Goodman, shot by a cop for nothing. He hadn't done anything, didn't the lawman know that? Why did he keep shooting? Why wouldn't he stop? He screamed. "Please stop! Oh, my God, please stop!"

There was no new pain, but the wounds had hurt him worse than anything he had ever known before. He looked over his shoulder as he tried to drag himself into the barn. His legs wouldn't work. They were just dead weight, objects dragging along behind his torso and slowing him down. His vision blurred, and he could feel cold sweat running down his face. But now the cop was coming, running at him. His revolver was still in his outstretched arm, and he was yelling something that Dennis couldn't comprehend. He could hear the words, but with the level of pain, they didn't mean anything.

Then the deputy was there, standing over him. The gun, with a barrel the size of a water pipe, was pointed straight into Goodman's eyes. The man holding it was angry. His teeth were clenched, his arms locked at the elbows.

The deputy was screaming. "You son of a bitch, I told you to stop. Lay still, or I'll finish you."

Goodman screamed back, yelling as loudly as he could through the pain. "You bastard, I'm one of the hostages. The killers are inside. You son of a bitch! Why'd you shoot me?"

The cold look left the deputy's face. Where it had been there was now terror. "What the hell are you talking about? Who are you?"

"Dennis Goodman. I'm with Caryn Collins."

"The singer? You lost your mind? Caryn Collins ain't here . . . is she?"

"In the house. Prison escapees. They took us hostage. All of us."

"Oh, shit! I'll get us some help. Don't move. I'll—"

The deputy never finished what he was saying. A loud sporadic chatter from a submachine gun came from the direction of the house. The lawman's body trembled as if he had touched a live electrical wire, and then he collapsed on the ground beside Goodman. His fingers twitched for a moment, stopped moving, and then his body remained motionless.

Dennis pried the fallen man's revolver from limp fingers. He swung the cylinder open. Three rounds remained unfired. He looked on the guy's gunbelt for more ammo. There were two leather dump pouches with six rounds in each. The cartridge cases from one of the pouches had corroded to a greenish haze from the leather salts. And from that observation, Goodman knew there was no telling how old the ammo was. He wasn't sure the ammo would chamber in the cylinder. Worse yet, there was no telling if it would fire.

More gunfire. Dirt sprayed around him, and Goodman slammed his face down to protect his eyes. He wriggled and crawled until he had the body of the slain deputy between him and the source of the gunfire.

He could see it now. It came from the window he had jumped through. He could tell it was Lionel Lewis, leaning against the window frame, firing the submachine gun even as his life's blood trickled away.

More deadly projectiles chewed the earth in front of the slain deputy and carved a path to the man's body. Goodman could hear the loud, sickening thuds when the bullets found flesh and rocked the dead man.

Goodman twisted his head so he could see the barn doors. They were little more than ten feet away. He decided to chance it. His trembling right hand moved the revolver over the dead deputy's chest. He leveled the gun at the house, but he aimed just right of where Lewis was standing. The old revolver was in poor repair, and Goodman had to strain to get the hammer back to full cock. With gentle pressure on the trigger from his trembling finger, Goodman tapped off a single round. He heard the bullet slap into the wooden structure of the house, and Lionel Lewis vanished from sight.

Goodman struggled to make his legs move. He crawled on his elbows, dragging his aching legs toward the barn. Three shots rang out, and then the shooting stopped.

Dennis knew it was now or never. He strained, pulled, and clawed at the ground until he reached the doors. His left arm pulled at the ragged wooden doors until one of them finally moved enough for him to get through. When he was satisfied that he could clear the opening, he forced his damaged body to move inside.

Goodman reached to the door once more and pulled it closed as best he could. He held the revolver tightly in his right hand and allowed his body to relax ever so slightly on the barn's earthen floor.

He took a few deep breaths to try to relax and flush himself of the breathtaking pain. He was breathing hard, the air burning as it entered his lungs. He told himself to relax, to calm down. For a long moment, it worked. Then his body snapped tensely to alert when he heard the sound behind him, inside the barn.

The atmosphere inside the house had suddenly changed from nerve-racking to chaotic with the sound of the first gunshots. In the room where Caryn Collins and the other hostages were held, Lionel Lewis fumbled with another magazine for the little Ingram MAC-10 9mm submachine gun. He had fired-out the first stick in the confrontation with Mike Coble, then at the deputy and Dennis Goodman.

Lewis was fighting to retain consciousness. Darkness came over him in sweeping, erratic waves. But even as he ascended from the oscillating waves of darkness, he felt his body weakening. His fingers were numb, and he hurt like hell. Three rounds from the subgun had raked his side when Coble had tried to disarm him. Judging by the way he hurt, Lewis figured the bullets had, at the very least, broken some of his ribs. The torn wounds in his flesh were superficial, and he would live, but they hurt, burned, and bled badly.

Lionel leaned harder against the wall to support his weight and keep himself from falling to the floor. He wanted to call to the others for help, but he knew better, because Richie and Ray wouldn't tolerate weakness. They would rather guard the hostages themselves than risk having one of their own overpowered by the captives. They would also figure if he was stupid enough to get himself shot, then he was too stupid to live. And that meant they would just as soon kill him and get him out of their way; that was standard prison operating procedure—inside or outside the walls. Whatever the reason for weakness, only the strong survived.

Bernie Aldridge was scared shitless because things had really gone haywire. He knelt beside Caryn Collins and Marilee Evans while they attempted to tend Mike Coble's wounds. The other members of the group stood frozen around the room. Bernie firmly expected one or more of the other crazed kidnappers to come sailing through the door with their guns spitting death. Aldridge looked away from Coble, who was bleeding profusely. His eyes locked with Danny St. John's, another of the stage crew, then drifted off to Lionel Lewis. Aldridge could tell

Lewis was hurting badly by the way he stood and the trickle of blood that saturated the gunman's shirt.

St. John turned his head slowly until Lewis was in full view. He stared at the shooter for a moment, then looked back at Bernie. He nodded slightly in the direction of Lewis and raised his hands into a position that simulated a choking movement.

Aldridge acknowledged with a slight nod of his head.

St. John moved forward one small cautious step at a time until he was within striking distance of Lewis, who still had his back to the captives.

Lewis continued to fumble with the 9-mm magazine, missing with each try at seating it into the well. Finally, he connected the parts, and the magazine slipped into position. He moved his hand, nudged the charging lever backward, and let it slam forward. The top round stripped from the magazine and slapped into the chamber. With the MAC-10 ready to spit death, Lewis turned back toward the captives.

Danny St. John lunged. His hands aimed for Lionel Lewis's neck and found their mark. Lewis was stunned, but he jerked the trigger on the subgun. The room vibrated with the staccato of the roaring weapon, but the shots slammed harmlessly into the wooden floor. The captives covered their ears with their hands against the deafening sound, and most of them screamed. Lionel's face turned from medium brown to crimson red as St. John squeezed with all of his strength. St. John hit the subgun with his knee, attempting to deflect the muzzle away from him. Lewis let the muzzle drop slightly, and a burst of 9-mm slugs ripped through St. John's left foot.

St. John screamed, his face grimaced with pain, but he didn't loosen his death grip. Lewis's eyes bulged, and the veins in his head protruded. The black shooter struggled for breath while his finger worked the Ingram's trigger back and forth in reflex motions that produced short, sporadic bursts of gunfire.

St. John squeezed with everything he had, but Lewis was tougher than he had expected, and he wouldn't go down. St. John released his grip and came back with his right fist to launch a jab. Lewis managed to get the weapon pointed into St. John's abdomen and squeeze the trigger. A single round roared, and the death pellet struck Danny St. John just below the sternum. He fell backwards, his body trembling from the massive impact. Then his knees buckled, and he slumped to the floor.

Lewis was choking, trying to get air into his body. He waved the muzzle of the submachine gun around the room with his right hand, pointing it at first one hostage, then another. His left hand stayed on his throat, rubbing it. He managed to get enough air into his lungs to speak. "Any more of you honky mothers wanna be dead heroes?"

Lilly Arthur answered the deputy sheriff's knock at the door an instant before the gunfire started in the room where Lionel Lewis guarded the prisoners. She froze, her head down in the same position as when she had descended the stairs. Halloway had abandoned his plans to go out the back of the house, and he could hear her mumbling something, but he couldn't tell what it was. He thought it was a prayer, and if it was, she was certainly going to need it because all she had left was a prayer. Maybe.

The deputy sheriff was too stunned to react. A large man who appeared to be in his fifties, the lawman just stood there as if he were trying to make a decision whether to rush into the house or run. He ran.

Richie Halloway ran for the door and shoved Lilly Arthur out of the way. He stepped through the door, sweeping the area in front of him with the barrel of his shotgun.

The deputy saw Halloway first and fired a single shot with his service revolver. The bullet missed and slammed into the front wall of the house beside Richie's head. Wood splinters flew in a stinging spray that sent chips down Halloway's shirtcollar.

Richie ducked back through the doorway, screaming, "Ray, get your ass down here. Dammit, Ray, where the hell are you?"

There was no answer.

"Okay, old woman. Get on the floor in front of the

sofa. You as much as move your head, and I'll blow it off. Now get down there."

Lilly Arthur reluctantly moved to the sofa and never looked at Halloway. She lay on the floor, praying aloud. "Oh, Lord, deliver me from these evil men. Take me home, but deliver me from these sinful workers of the devil."

Lilly's prayers angered Halloway. "Shut up, you bitch."

Lilly Arthur was unmoved. She kept praying, repeating the same words over and over.

"Dammit, old woman, I mean it. Shut the hell up."

Lilly paid no attention to the gun-wielding sinner. She kept praying, but now her prayers were louder.

"Shit!" Halloway turned back to the window where he had last seen the deputy. He raised his shotgun to his hip and scanned the yard outside. "Ray! Dammit, Ray, answer me!"

Ray didn't answer Halloway because he didn't hear him. At the sound of the first burst of gunfire, Hartley had retreated to the second floor of the house. He stood in what had been Mary Beth's bedroom nine years before but was now Lilly Arthur's prison. He had cautiously looked out the window toward the barn and watched as Lionel Lewis shot the man from Caryn Collins's entourage and then wasted the deputy sheriff. He knew there was another lawman lurking somewhere near the front of the house. The pistol shot had told him that much.

Nine years in prison had transformed Ray Hartley into a cold, calculating terminator of human life. Since the night he had cradled the dead body of the only person he had ever loved in his arms, Ray Hartley had felt no more remorse about taking the life of another human being than he felt about squashing a bug. And as he stood beside the window, Hartley was cold-hearted and methodical. He laid his plan to terminate the remaining deputy sheriff.

Hartley unlatched the window and slid the bottom section of the window upward. He kicked the screen out and climbed through. His feet landed on the sloping surface of a roof that covered the porch at the back and side of the house. Hartley moved down the roof toward the edge, crouching in a duckwalk. He cradled the shotgun on his lap, his finger resting on the trigger. When he reached the edge of the roof, he stopped and stared at the ground below. The best he could determine, it was seven or eight feet to solid ground. And beyond that, twenty-five yards in the direction of the barn, sat the springhouse. If he could hit the ground running, Hartley calculated, there would be three or four seconds in the clear until he reached cover. If the deputy saw him and could shoot straight, he might not make it. But if he could reach the springhouse, he would be behind the lawman, and that was what he wanted.

Hartley jumped. He hit the ground hard and immediately fell into a tuck-and-roll to diminish the impact. His motion never stopped from the time he landed on the grass until he scrambled to his feet and set out in a dead run toward the springhouse. Hartley's right hand was firmly wrapped around the pistol grip of the shotgun. The recesses of his mind waited for a thunderous roar or a searing pain from the deputy's weapon as he ran, but it didn't come. It took less than the four seconds he had anticipated to reach the safety of the springhouse. Hartley slid to a stop at the back wall of the little wooden building. The short run had winded him, and he struggled to breathe. Once he caught his breath, he leaned around the edge of the wall and looked for the deputy.

He saw the lawman, crouched down at the front corner of the house. His back was a clear shot from where Hartley sat. Ray raised the shotgun with one hand and leveled the bead squarely on the deputy's back, but he was still unsteady because of the run. He lowered the gun and worked to regulate his breathing. This was no time for a screwup. The lawman had to fall with the first shot.

After two minutes, Hartley raised the shotgun again. This time, his breathing was steady, his aim true. He had already punched the safety off when he made the jump, so he eased back on the trigger. "Bye, lawman. See you in hell."

A shotgun blast rang out, and the deputy crouched more firmly against the house. Hartley released the pressure on the trigger. "Damn you, Richie. Another second, and the mother would have been mine." The words came out in a whisper, and Hartley lowered the shotgun. He had to know what Richie was firing at. He knew Halloway couldn't see the deputy from inside the house. The only thing he could figure was that Richie had fired simply to distract the deputy.

The lawman sat firm, looking first at the front porch and then toward his patrol car. He kept his revolver poised in his right hand, ready. Without any warning, the deputy stood and bolted in a hard run toward the patrol car. Ten feet from the front of the house, he cracked off two rounds through the front window, as a distraction.

Ray came up with the shotgun fast. He let the barrel settle until the bead sat squarely into the running lawman's back. He nudged the trigger to the rear, and the recoil shoved him backward. He jacked the empty from the chamber and slammed another round up the tube. He was up and running before the empty shell hit the ground.

Ahead of him now, the lawman was down on the ground. He was kicking, rolling, and screaming. His arms flapped without direction like the wings of a wounded bird. In seconds, Hartley stood beside the fallen deputy. The instant the wounded lawman saw Hartley, he froze. Blood oozed from his lips, and the effect of several 00-buckshot pellets showed in patches of blood that seeped through the lawman's uniform. His open hand strained to reach his service revolver that lay only inches from the bloody tips of his fingers.

Hartley's face was cold and vacant. "No, no, pigman. Not this time."

The deputy's eyes were wide with terror. He struggled to get air into his pain-ravaged body. His fingers stopped moving. "Who are you?" Even before he asked the question, he knew.

Hartley was grinning now. He held the shotgun with one hand and pointed it directly at the officer's fear-laden face. "Nine years ago, up in the hills. You're the bastard that led the posse. Remember me now?"

The deputy's face was a mixture of fear and dismay. "Hartley... Ray Hartley."

"Yeah, Jesse, Ray Hartley. It's been a long time. Remember how you and one of your deputies beat the hell out of me when you finally captured me up in those hills? Remember?"

The lawman didn't answer. His eyes opened even wider.

"This is a bonus. I'd sort of let that one slip past me, Jesse."

"What are you gonna do to me? Have you hurt Miss Lilly?"

"Miss Lilly ain't hurt. Not yet, anyway. Her time's coming real soon. Your time's come now, Jesse. The way I see it, I got two choices. I can let you lay here and bleed to death real slow, or I can splatter your brains all over this yard. But you see, my problem is I don't have a lot of time. What do you think, Jesse?"

"Hartley, you're crazy. I should have killed you up in the hills. It would've saved the taxpayers a hell of a lot of money. You're trash, Hartley, nothin' but common garbage. Time's comin' when you'll get yours."

Ray Hartley's face split into a broad smile. "Yeah, maybe I am and maybe I will, but you'll never know. You see, you're dead, Jesse." Hartley pushed the barrel of the Remington to within six inches of the bridge of Jesse's nose.

The lawman's eyes opened wider than the bore of the twelve-gauge they stared into.

Hartley applied pressure to the trigger. "Bye, lawman."

CHAPTER TEN

Roy O'Connall had been following Cliff Scott and his female companion for over an hour. They had gone to a sporting-goods store and left with a large quantity of what appeared to be small-arms ammunition. After that, they had visited two grocery stores. O'Connall waited now in the busy parking lot of a third grocery store. The haul at the first two stores appeared to be enough to feed a small army. And now, with the couple shopping in a third food store, Roy wondered if perhaps that was just what they intended to feed—a small army... or perhaps a small group of hostages.

O'Connall realized that Scott would have been easy meat to take down at any time since the verbal exchange with his female companion at Air Equipment. But that choice wouldn't lead him where he wanted to go—to Caryn Collins and the stolen buses. Roy decided that when the time came, he would take Scott quickly. If the fugitive cooperated, he could return to prison. If he didn't, well, whatever had to be done would be done. He would simply play it by ear. The ultimate choice of Cliff Scott's fate rested with Cliff Scott. The hell of it was, the guy probably didn't realize it.

Scott and his companion had been in the store for a little over five minutes. If their shopping spree lasted as long as the previous two, Roy figured he had at least another ten minutes. He fired the engine on the Vette and moved to a pay telephone across the parking lot. He checked it out before he moved and determined that he would have no trouble watching the exit doors or the van while he made a call.

He dropped his last quarter into the slot and dialed a collect call to Jimmy Franklin. After the normal routine of irate disgust, Franklin finally accepted the call.

"Jimmy, my main man. What have you got for me?"

Franklin's voice was hostile. "One hell of a bill, that's what. But that's only starters."

Roy laughed. "Now, Jimmy, watch the attitude. Haven't I always paid you?"

"I'd rather not get into that on my nickel. This one's gonna cost you dearly, O'Connall. This is heavy shit."

"I'm listening. Speak to me."

"Okay, I put out some feelers. I got some ears and feet working together on the street. The buzz on the pavement is real interesting."

"Okay, Jimmy. That sounds nice. What about the insurance? You find out anything for me on the insurance?"

"Patience, my nuisance friend. All things come in time. You know, Roy, that's one of your major problems. You got too little patience. You need to work on that."

"Can the psychotherapy. What about the insurance?"

"The broad's got insurance all right. Loads of it. Ten mill to be exact."

O'Connall almost choked. "Ten million dollars in life insurance? No shit?"

"That's the straight stuff, O'Connall. This broad has made some bucks in her time, but she's worth a hell of a lot more dead than alive. To some folks at least."

"Like who?"

"Two entities. Both of 'em are close to her. One holds eight million on her through Lloyd's of London. The other has two mill on her."

O'Connall watched the store exit as he talked. "Interesting. Who is it?"

"Well, I done a little checking, you see. The fat boy that's holding the eight mill is in deep financial shit. He was a real fat cat for a while, but he's apparently snorted it or gambled it or something, 'cause it's all gone. The sharks and the gators want a piece of his ass. The hell of it is, he's personally clean. Not a black credit marker against him.

All the shit that's failed to flush has piled up in two or three businesses. He's a slick asshole, and I don't think Caryn Collins's management company knows he's set them on the financial line."

O'Connall listened intently. "All right, already. So speak to me. Who's trying to tarnish the glitter of Caryn Collins's shining star?"

Jimmy Franklin spoke fast, and Roy O'Connall listened, never letting his eyes drift from the front door of the store or Cliff Scott's van. After five minutes, Jimmy Franklin's voice slowed. "That's about it, O'Connall. When can I expect you to send money?"

"As soon as this case is in wraps, I'll be paying you a social call. You have my word on it. Thanks for everything."

"Hey, listen here, O'Connall. Social calls I don't need, and your word doesn't excite me. Money excites me. You got that?" Jimmy realized he was talking to a dead connection. "O'Connall? Dammit, Roy! Where the hell are you? You son of a bitch! O'Connall! Operator! Shit!" Jimmy slammed the telephone down.

Roy heard Jimmy's voice squeaking through the receiver all the way back to the cradle. He laughed out loud and gently let the receiver slide into its holder. "I wonder," he whispered. He slapped the telephone coin box and heard a tinkling sound. His index finger swept through the coin-return door and landed on a pile of loose change. He slid the coins into the palm of his hand and counted them. "What do you know about that? A buck-sixty-five. Some days you're just too good, Roy." He pocketed the change and realized he had taken his eyes off of the van. He jerked his head up, quickly focusing on the van. The doors were open, and Scott and his companion were loading more groceries into it. O'Connall watched every move the pair made. It took two or three minutes before they were finished.

Roy followed the pair to a service station. They filled the tank, checked the oil, and soon they were rolling on the highway. Roy noticed a sign as they left the North Platte city limit that indicated they were traveling north on U.S. 83. O'Connall maintained a sufficient distance to assure that Scott wasn't aware that he was being followed.

He settled back in the comfortable Corvette seat and laid the Colt Python on the console. "Come on, pussycat. Take me to the lion's den."

———

Dennis Goodman thought he had reached safety inside the barn. As he struggled to recover from the wounds that had sent him reeling into pain and agony, the noise from the back part of the barn scared him senseless again. He managed to crawl to one of the tractor-trailer rigs parked inside. He got to the front tire and took cover behind it. The sound kept coming, sporadic and indistinct, but coming nonetheless. Something was moving cautiously and working its way to the front of the weathered wooden structure. Goodman managed to perch the slain deputy's revolver on his legs and waited. The sound of more gunfire from the house unnerved Goodman. Judging from the intensity and resonance of the roars, the last shot came from a shotgun. And that didn't sound too good. If his ears hadn't failed him, Goodman figured the other deputy had also bought it. And that was even worse.

Right now, dead cops were the least of Dennis Goodman's concerns. Right now, he wondered who or what was moving through the barn. He concentrated on survival, pure and simple. And the next detriment to his personal survival and the survival of every member of the Caryn Collins troupe was the unidentified sound coming in his direction with the skill and cunning of a cat. Goodman knew that if he didn't find a way to survive and a means of escape, it was very unlikely that any of the other captives in Lilly Arthur's farmhouse would live to relay the horror of their ordeal. And he'd be damned before he'd allow that to happen.

The sound came again, closer this time, slow and methodical. Goodman could tell that whatever it was took each step with acute sensitivity to its surroundings. If the sound came from a man, it could spell disaster. Worse than that, it could very well mean death. And Dennis Goodman wasn't ready to die without putting up one hell of a fight.

The source of the sound was near the end of the

eighteen-wheeler he was using for cover. It came now from somewhere near the end of the trailer. Goodman eased the hammer back on the old unkempt revolver, took a deep breath, and waited for something to shoot. His heart raced, and that intensified the pain from his cuts and gunshot wounds. He was losing blood fast, and he could feel both strength and life oozing from his body with every beat of his heart. He had to get to the first-aid kit on the bus to find something to treat himself. Only one obstacle stood between him and treatment, and it was at the other end of the over-road eighteen-wheel rig.

Goodman bit his lips and waited. He tried to ignore the pain, but now the burning was worse. He could sense his vision blurring and fading. Then he reached down inside himself for all the strength and willpower he had stored over a lifetime. He found a new burst of energy from a raw survival instinct just as the source of the sound stepped into the clear beside the rig. At the sight, Goodman squeezed on the revolver's trigger, but a voice from behind him made him stop.

"You just ease that gun to the ground, young feller. That gun goes off and hurts my cat, and I'll lay this here ax right square through the top of your head."

Dennis let the gun slip gently down the side of his legs. The cat that had been the source of his panic walked off across the barn's earthen floor and disappeared through an opening in the barn wall. Goodman ventured a slow twist of his head to get a look at the man behind him.

"No, I wouldn't do that. Don't turn around just yet. I just sharpened this here ax last week. It's fine enough to split a hen's hair, and it'll do the same through you like short work."

Goodman let the gun rest on the ground. "Who are you?"

"Reckon I'll do the askin' and you do the answerin', seein' as how I got this ax perched over your noggin. Who are you, and what are all these here trucks and buses doin' in Miss Lilly's barn?"

"We've all been kidnapped by some maniac prison escapees. They brought us here. Look, I'm hurt pretty bad. I need to get to some bandages and stuff in one of the buses. Will you help me?"

"Depends. Where's Miss Lilly and her farmhands?"

"She's in the house, or she was when I ran from there a little while ago. The farmhands are dead. Both of 'em. These men killed them when we came to the farm a few days ago."

"What'd them fellers do with the dead hands?"

"I don't know. They locked us up inside. We haven't seen or heard too much since then. Well, that is until the sheriff's deputies came a little while ago. I think they're both dead now."

"If you be lyin' to me, boy, I'll whack your head off like a Sunday fryin' hen. You hear me?"

"I swear, Mister, I'm not lyin'. If you aren't one of those kidnappin' dirtbags, I got no quarrel with you. I need your help."

"I'm alistenin'."

"Who are you anyway?"

"Name's Wilbur Matthews. It be my farm what joins Miss Lilly's over on the far side. I've not heard nothin' from over here in a coupla days, and I sorta got myself concerned. Thought I might come snoopin' to see what was agoin' on. I seen that sheriff's car, and then I heared them gunshots. Figured I'd come through the barn and take me a look-see without nobody aseein'. When I seen all these here trucks and stuff and then I seen you with that pistol, well, I kinda figured maybe you and me needed to have a little talk. You know what I mean?"

"Well, Wilbur, I'm glad you came. You help me, and maybe between the two of us we can help Miss Lilly. We might be able to save her life. There's a man in there named Ray Hartley that wants mighty badly to kill Miss Lilly, best I can determine."

"Jesus, help us all, boy, are you sure? Ray Hartley is in that house right now?"

"He was when I left. Will you help me?"

"My shootin' iron is over on the far side of the hill in my pickup truck. What is it you want me to do?"

Dennis Goodman breathed a sigh of relief. "Okay, Wilbur, I need a first-aid kit from inside one of the buses.

There should be one right behind the driver's seat. And we've got a gun stashed in a toolbox on board. We need to get to that too. It may be the only chance the people in that farmhouse have to see tomorrow. We got to hurry, Wilbur. I'm shot pretty bad. I can tell you what to do, but I don't know how much I can do for myself."

Wilbur put the ax down and for the first time, Dennis Goodman turned around and looked at the man. He was every day of sixty. His stringy hair was white, and bony fingers shot from beneath his baseball-style cap like nettles on a cactus. Wilbur's face was hard, dry, and etched in craterlike patterns that resembled roadways on a topographical map. He had two missing teeth near the front, and the remaining teeth that Goodman could see were tarnished by tobacco juice. The old guy wore a faded flannel shirt and bib overalls, despite the moderate weather. In the breastpockets of Wilbur's well-worn overalls, Goodman could see the imprint of a wallet on one side and a plug of chewing tobacco on the other.

Wilbur looked over Dennis Goodman's wounds. "Young feller, what're we gonna do once I got you patched up? With them legs the way they are, you ain't gonna be too good for nothin'."

"Wilbur, I'm going to give you a crash course in bus driving and we're going to go call the police."

"Was they two of 'em over yonder at the house? Two sheriffs?"

"Yes, why?"

"Ain't gonna do no good to call the sheriff. Them two fellers are all they is. We only got two lawmen in this here county. Never need no more 'cept when Ray Hartley busts loose on a rampage."

———

Thedford, Nebraska, was a sleepy little settlement near the edge of the Nebraska National Forest. Marc and Carl wondered how a place so painted in natural beauty and so peaceful could have had a neighbor like Ray Hartley. Lilly Arthur's farm, according to the information furnished by Brittin Crain, lay in the fertile sand hills just north of the Middle Loup River outside Thedford. The network of small connecting roads were hardly suitable for the massive Leeco over-road rig. Negotiable, yes; prudently suitable, no.

Marc and Carl agreed to drop the rig and move in for their initial inspection of the farm by using one of the custom Jeep Cherokees. The rig traveling along rural roadways would in all likelihood attract unnecessary attention. The presence of a Cherokee four-by-four, on the other hand, wouldn't be unusual.

The most logical place to leave the rig was the local Farm Cooperative. The large gravel parking area was quite sufficient for a machine the size of a Leeco rig. Once they had stopped at the Co-op, both men went in and spoke with the management. They explained the nature of their business by using a bit of creative improvisation. For cover, Marc and Carl assumed the role of an agricultural survey team sent in by the federal government to determine what aid, if any, the local cattle farmers required. It worked—the management expressed a willingness to help in any way they could.

Once the red Cherokee was unloaded from the mighty Leeco war machine, Marc transferred all of the data stored in the eighteen-wheeler's on-board computer into the memory bank of the portable computer system in the red Cherokee. The map display and satellite tracking system checked out flawlessly. After a rapid check of their complement of necessary arms and ammunition, the highway warriors set out for Lilly Arthur's farm. And with the computer tracking system in place, finding it was as simple as following a beacon in the night.

The highway warriors had decided to approach the farm from the rear rather than driving recklessly into the mouth of the alligator. Hostage rescue had been one of their specialties during their extended tenure in Delta Force. But extraction, even under the very best of circumstances, was an extremely risky business. The perpetrators of violent abduction usually lived by the philosophy that they had nothing left to lose. And if an extraction team was accidently detected prior to reaching its intended target, that could spell an immediate death sentence for the captives.

Carl wove the Cherokee through the narrow country backroads while Marc navigated by following the blip on the computer screen. Carl was the first to break the silence. "What's the plan if we find the scumbags there?"

Marc looked away from the computer screen and stared out the window at the lush sandy grasslands. "I figure we do a thorough recon first. If we find anything that indicates Collins or the escapees are here, we'll wait until dark and make a move. Maybe something like we used in El Salvador that time we hit the terrorist training camp and got the American advisor out."

"Yeah, that could be workable. Those shitheads never knew what happened until we were in and gone. But there's only two of us this time. We had five men on that one, and it was one hell of a plan. There was also an elite Delta Force unit in Cobra gunships two miles away. We don't have that kind of luxury this time."

"We can handle it. These guys have been confined for a long time. They're scared shitless, and none of them show a record of military training. Any opposition they could give us would be just down-and-dirty street fighting. That never has been and never will be a match for what we learned in Delta Force. I think they're just hard-core dirtbags, and if that's the case, we'll be the broom that sweeps them away. I don't think they'll be too bad unless they had additional support join their ranks after the breakout. The important thing is to get Caryn Collins and her people to safety, but right now, we're playing on pure speculation."

Carl tightened his grip on the steering wheel. He glanced at Marc, then immediately took his eyes back to the winding road. "We're at a substantial disadvantage. We don't have any intelligence to operate from. All we know is there's a farm and some little old woman lives there alone. If there are houses or buildings, we've got no layout. If we have to wing it, that'll make the nut harder to crack."

Marc nodded in agreement. "One advantage we do have is the element of surprise. If they're there, we know we're going in; they don't. If the atmosphere looks conducive, we can try to get the hostages out and then deal with the captors. If it isn't conducive, then we'll deal with the bastards as the situation warrants. They don't want to play the game our way, and we'll see to it that they end up being just one more giant sack of shit flushed down the commode of life. But then there is always one other possibility."

"What's that?"

"These dirtbags could have come here, done their dirty work, and already split. And there is also the possibility they never came here in the first place. For slime like Hartley, it would be too damned obvious."

Carl took the Cherokee through a hairpin curve and straightened it out. The road seemed to become narrower with each passing mile. "Yeah, but people like him have lost the ability to think, to reason things out. If he hadn't already lost that, he wouldn't have done what he did. Rationally thinking people don't commit cold-blooded murder. It takes a hard heart or an angry one to do that sort of thing."

Marc was adamant. "Judging from the records Brittin sent us, I think Ray Hartley and his companions qualify either way. I'm not even sure any of them have a heart anymore. The very nature of their crimes proves they're all hard-core leeches. The system couldn't handle them . . . maybe we can."

CHAPTER ELEVEN

Richie Halloway had ducked back into the room where Lionel Lewis stood guard the instant he saw the lawman fall to the ground from Hartley's shotgun blast. The downed deputy and the report of the shotgun immediately answered the question of why Ray hadn't responded when he had yelled for him earlier. Deep inside, it made him smile to think he was in the company of someone as competent as Hartley. After all, his confidence in Hartley's ability was one of the reasons he had selected him.

Lionel Lewis was a different story. When Halloway saw Lionel was shot, his first reaction was to yell at him. When your survival depended on competence, incompetence couldn't be tolerated. And if Lionel hadn't been incompetent, he wouldn't have gotten himself shot. Halloway reevaluated the situation and realized he was shorthanded enough as it was; otherwise, he would have finished the job the captives started. He decided to console Lewis as best he could. He looked the slender black guy over and decided he could still handle the job of guarding Collins and her employees.

Halloway hit the front porch on the run. He ran to Hartley and stopped. He took one look at the dead deputy, turned away, and vomited.

Ray Hartley laughed every time Halloway heaved his guts up. "Awesome what a load of twelve-gauge double-ought backshot will do to a man's face, huh, Richie?"

Halloway looked at Hartley. Richie's face was pale white. He wiped his mouth with his shirtsleeve and tried to speak but heaved again.

"Damn, Rich, I thought you had a stomach for killing. You turnin' soft on me?"

Halloway spit, wiped his face again, and looked back at Hartley. "Killin's one thing. Mutilation is another. The son of a bitch doesn't even have a head."

Hartley laughed again. "Ain't no big deal. He never had much of one before I blew it off."

"Tell me one thing, Ray. Was it necessary? I mean *really* necessary?"

"You want to spend the rest of your life in the joint?"

"What do you think?"

"All right, then. It was necessary."

"But I saw this man go down. He would have bled to death. Did you have to do *this* to him?"

"I believe in efficiency, Rich. I screwed up once and it landed me in the joint. I won't let it happen again."

"I just don't believe it. Look at this guy."

"Shit, Rich. I thought you had some guts."

Halloway slammed the barrel of his shotgun into Hartley's throat. "Listen to me, shit-for-brains. I got guts, and I can kill with the best of 'em. What you did with a shotgun in this man's face goes beyond killin'. Now if you don't want a load of the same thing, you just shut the hell up. You hear me?"

Hartley's face was blank. He felt the blood rushing from his head, and he suddenly felt weak. "All right, all right. Settle down, Rich. I was just havin' a little fun with you, that's all. I didn't mean nothin' by it."

"Okay. You just keep your jaws shut, and me and you will get along fine. When this is over, you can go your way, and I'll go mine. Until then, just shut up."

Halloway lowered the shotgun and let it drop to his side. "Okay, Ray, what do you plan on doing with these two cops?"

"We gotta get rid of 'em. Can't leave 'em here."

"Get rid of the cop car, too. When these two guys don't check back in, somebody's gonna come lookin'."

"I don't think we have to worry about that for a while. When I lived around here, there weren't but two lawmen.

The sheriff, that's old Jesse here, and one deputy. Unless things have changed, I don't suspect there's more than two now."

"It coulda changed by now."

Hartley laughed again. "You don't understand, Rich. Thomas County ain't somewhere people move *to,* it's somewhere you move *from.* Most of these old farmers been here for generations. Some of their kids grow up and move to the big city, but most of 'em that were born here die here."

"I don't need a history lesson. I just want to do something with these bodies and that patrol car. There's no more room in the barn."

"Yeah, but there's another body in the barn."

Halloway tensed with excitement. "What?"

"One of Collins's people made a run for it. The deputy out by the barn iced him. He was hit bad. I could tell by the way he moved. He crawled off into the barn. I figure we can give him a little while, and he'll be bled to death."

"Shit! Lionel didn't tell me that. No wonder he got himself shot."

"He's shot?"

"Yeah, flesh wounds. He'll be all right, but he's hurtin' like hell. He killed one of the hostages too. Cut another one pretty bad."

"Damn. We can't have a bunch of dead bodies layin' around. I know a place about half a mile west of here. It's a hollow hole in the sand hills. Wind blowed it out so now it's like a cave. Been there since I was a kid. It's big enough to drive a car in. We can load all the bodies up in the trunk of the car, and I'll take it over there and leave it. I can go back tonight and set fire to it. Nobody'll ever be able to see it inside the sandhole."

"You drag this bloody pulp out behind the house, and then we can get the other one out by the barn. I'll drive the car around back and leave it there until Cliff gets back. He can help us load the bodies."

Hartley nodded. "Okay, Rich. What then?"

Halloway spit once more and cleared his throat. "I'm thinkin' maybe tonight after you set fire to the car, we ought to load all these people up and leave this place. I'm worried more cops're comin'. And next time it might be more than two."

Hartley laughed. "If the others that come are as stupid as these two, let 'em come."

"Don't underestimate cops, Ray. They nailed our butts once, didn't they?"

Ray Hartley had no answer.

———

Dennis Goodman felt like two-thirds of his body was on fire. But despite the pain, he was still rational enough to realize he was getting weaker with every beat of his heart. Wilbur was probably a very good farmer, but his medical skills left a lot to be desired. Goodman thought he would bleed himself into unconsciousness before the old farmer could get bandages on his wounds. He had four jagged lacerations from the shard of glass that had raked his shoulders and back when he'd jumped from the broken window. The gunshot wounds in his leg and hip intensified the searing pain.

Goodman fought to regulate his breathing, which he hoped would lessen the pain. Each time old Wilbur placed a gauze compress from the first-aid kit on one of the open wounds, Goodman flinched and gritted his teeth. He thought numbness would soon set in and dull the pain, but no dice. After twenty minutes that seemed like twenty hours, Wilbur told Goodman he had bandaged all the wounds. He had multilayered several of the bleeding areas in an effort to stop or at least slow the bleeding.

For the first time, Dennis Goodman realized just how uncomfortable the bunks on the buses were. Of course, it didn't help that he had been required to lie on his stomach so Wilbur could treat the wounds. He managed to roll over and let his feet drop to the floor. He held tightly to the rail of the bunk and managed to stand. It had always been standard procedure to keep an extra set of keys to each vehicle in every vehicle on the tour.

Dennis searched the front lockbox for the keys to the storage bin on the show bus. He found them and gave the proper key to Wilbur. "This will open the second bin from the back of the bus on the right side. Inside, you'll find a red toolbox. Open it with this key. Under the top tray in the box is a brown cardboard box. If you look inside of it, there should be a nine-millimeter automatic pistol and a couple of extra clips. Get 'em and bring 'em back. While you're doing that, I'm going to try to get a call out on the cellular telephone. Can you handle that?"

Wilbur nodded. He turned, although slowly, and climbed down the steps from the passenger compartment of the bus.

Dennis sat in the lounge seat behind the driver's station. Every move he made hurt worse than he would have thought possible. He lifted the receiver on the cellular telephone and pushed the search activator. With a lot of luck, the little unit would lock onto a clear channel, and he could get help. A blinking light indicated the scanner was searching, but nothing happened. He picked up the receiver and pressed the transmit switch, hoping that would locate a signal. Still, nothing.

Several minutes passed with nothing but the blinking light on the handset and the sound of Wilbur fumbling through the storage bin beneath the floor of the bus. Goodman watched through glassy eyes, his vision fading in and out. When another minute had passed, he slammed the handset back into the cradle and let out a disgusted sigh. He jerked his head toward the door when he heard Wilbur start up the steps. "Oh, thank God, you found it."

Wilbur smiled, showing the five teeth he had left in his mouth. "You give right good directions. You know how to use one of these things, young feller?"

"Yeah, I can use it, and I damned sure will if I can get a shot at those assholes. You know how to use it?"

Wilbur laughed. "Me? Hell, no. I can shoot a gnat off a squirrel's ass with my little twenty-two, but one of these fandangled things . . . probly shoot myself with it."

"Well, Wilbur, you're about to learn. Hand it to me."

Wilbur passed the Smith & Wesson Model 59 to Goodman. "Here's them clips you was talkin' about, too."

Goodman took the old blue automatic in his weakening hands. His thumb hit the magazine release, and the faded blue magazine dropped to the lounge seat. He managed to get the slide back and eject the chambered round. He checked the barrel for obstructions; it was clear. Goodman used his thumb to press the top round back into the magazine, then checked the witness holes to be sure the mag was full. It was.

It took some effort, but Goodman finally got the magazine back into the well and shoved it home until it clicked. He pulled back the slide and chambered a round. "You watch me do all that, Wilbur?"

"Yeah, I did."

"Can you do that much?"

"If you'll tell me what all them buttons and levers are for."

"There are only three of them, Wilbur. The round one here releases the magazine. When you're shooting and you're empty, the slide will lock back. You have to put another one in it to fire again. You take the empty out by pressing this button, and then you put a loaded one in it. Next, take your thumb and push this slide lock on the side downward until the slide slams closed. Watch your hands when you do that. It can hurt you."

"All right, then what?"

Goodman pointed to the safety release. "This slide operates the safety tumbler. When it's down, it's safe. To fire, push it up with your thumb. After that, just aim and squeeze the trigger. The first round is double-action, so you don't have to cock it. After the first shot, it's a semiautomatic. This gun will shoot fifteen times with a full magazine and one in the chamber."

"Sounds pretty complicated to me."

"Not really. One thing to watch, though. Don't let the slide get your hand when you're shooting. It comes back and slams closed very fast when you fire a shot. It'll eat your hand up if you get one of 'em in the way. Hold it like this." Goodman held the auto out with both hands and showed Wilbur how to handle the weapon in his hands. "Now look, I may go out like a light anytime. I'm not feeling too good. Those people inside that house are countin' on you to get us all out of here alive."

"I could just go out the back way, the way I came in, and get my squirrel gun. I can handle them varmits with that. If'n I could get to my pickup truck, I could drive back over to the house and call the state police. They could get here within a hour or so in one of them hellycopters."

"I don't think I'll last that long." Dennis paused. "What was that?"

"What?"

"It sounded like a car engine. Someone's coming. Pull that lever and close the door. They can't get in if the door is closed. Help me back to the middle of the bus. That's the safest place. Hurry, Wilbur. They're close."

———

"Where the hell are you taking me?" Roy O'Connall was talking to himself again. "I worry about you, Roy. Pretty soon you'll start answering yourself. Not good."

Ahead of O'Connall's ZR-1 Corvette, Cliff Scott drove the blue Dodge van over the winding country backroads as if he had done it every day of his life. It became increasingly more difficult for O'Connall to keep clear of Scott's rearview. For the last five miles, the van and the Vette had been the only vehicles on the road. Worse than anything, the Vette just didn't fit in with the surroundings. The high-performance fire-engine-red Corvette contrasted against rolling fields of green wild grass and high-country farmland, and was about as inconspicuous as a hot-to-trot hooker at a salesman's convention.

O'Connall kept rubbing his left eye. The dust stirred up by the van found a way into the Vette and managed to contaminate his contact lens. The lens was a continual problem anyway. Some mornings he forgot to put it in; others, he was out of the solution that kept it moist. Every time he put the thing in his eye, he was reminded that he should have ducked the right hook that caused him to wear it. When the boxer had nailed him eight years before, the cut damaged a nerve, and that in turn necessitated wearing one contact to see where the hell he was going. Every time he failed to wear the thing, he was uncomfortably reminded by the dizziness that set in. After a while, the lens had become more of a nuisance than it was worth. Problem was, until he either went blind in the left eye or found a way to acquire a new one, the lens was the only option. Either way, in or out, the one contact lens was a frequent inconvenience, and right now was no exception.

Roy figured Cliff Scott and his female companion had to be either blind or stupid not to realize the Vette was behind them. The probability was made more interesting because Scott showed no signs of having detected the private investigator on his tail. But whatever the case, Roy decided to make the best of it as long as he could. He'd never been one to let stupidity slide unscathed when he could use it to his advantage. He lay back, relying more on the dust from the van's slipstream than actual visual contact with the rolling machine to determine where it had gone.

Roy topped a small knoll and noticed the cloud of dust in front of him slowing. He pulled off in the edge of a grassy field beside a row of scrub brush. Across the fields, he could see a farmhouse and several outbuildings sitting out in the middle of nowhere. Much to his surprise and more to his satisfaction, the van turned into a long winding lane that led to the farmhouse. Either Cliff Scott was stopping for fresh eggs, or Roy had just scored a home run. The farmhouse was a good quarter of a mile away, so Roy wasn't sure which it was.

Roy reached into the back storage compartment behind the seats and fumbled for his binoculars. He lifted them to his eyes. They were always a pain in the ass to use because of the imbalance in his vision. He manipulated the focusing ring on the right lens and then the center zoom focus. When he zeroed in on the front porch of the farmhouse, O'Connall realized he had scored a home run. Egg farmers didn't come out on the porch wielding sawed-off shotguns.

Roy eased the Vette into reverse and backed as slowly and quietly as he could down the blind side of the knoll away from the farmhouse. He did a fast turnaround and headed back the way he had come. There had been another small road that cut off through the fields less than a half mile back. He decided to take the Vette as far as it would go and hoof it the rest of the way. Right now, he wanted a closer look at the layout of the farm and its inhabitants.

The little road was right where he had remembered it. Roy pulled the Vette into the worn tractor path. The best he could determine, he was due east of the farmhouse. He drove several hundred yards until a deep ravine crossed the road. The low-slung Vette couldn't cross it. Roy stopped and shut the engine off. He removed the keys from the ignition, then unlocked the lid to the special false floor he had installed behind the seats. Once the lid was up, he removed his Ruger Mini-14 from a snug security rack.

A slight jerk opened the velcro closure to a long small box beneath the Ruger's rack. Roy lifted a Redfield telescopic sight from the box and slipped it in place on the Ruger. The little semiautomatic rifle had been highly customized by a gunsmith friend in St. Louis. The original wooden stock had been removed and replaced with a Ram Line synthetic folding stock. The gunsmith had installed a flash hider on the muzzle and a custom-made sixty-round butt-to-butt magazine from two thirty-round Federal Ordinance aftermarket mags. A special nonslip mounting system had been designed for the Redfield, so it could be mounted and dismounted without losing its previously sighted-in point of impact. The gunsmith had also made a second "jungle clip" (at least that's what he had called it) for the Mini. Roy always kept the magazines loaded with alternate rounds of 55-grain full-metal jacketed spire-points and 52-grain hollow-points. With a total of 120 rounds of potential death, Roy figured the little Mini amounted to a hell of a lot of firepower.

Roy wasn't looking for a firefight, but he didn't plan to get his ass shot off either. All he wanted right now was four escapees, Caryn Collins and her entourage, two show buses, and a paycheck from Interstate Leasing Services. The Mini-14 and the six-inch Colt Python .357 Magnum revolver could create great changes of heart for good old boys gone bad. And if it came down to a firefight . . . God help them.

Roy secured the Vette and headed off through the tall spiny grass. Fifty yards from the Vette, he decided that he would gladly trade his itching contact lens for a can of good insect repellent. Every bug around seemed hungry for a taste of his light fair skin. O'Connall kept moving despite the nagging pests. He had the Colt in the small of his back, the binoculars on a strap around his neck, and the Mini-14 on a nylon sling over his shoulder. In less than five minutes, he had topped the knoll, so the farmhouse came into full view.

From where Roy was, it looked like the barn lay due north of the farmhouse, to his right. There was also a little building he couldn't identify. It looked like a smokehouse or toolshed, but he couldn't tell. From his present angle, Roy couldn't see the entrance doors to the barn or the back of it. If he turned a few more yards north, he might get a better view. And if he could work his way through the chest-high grass to the barn without being detected, he'd have one great vantage point to start his silent attack on the murderous slimebags. One by one, he'd give them a chance to tell him where Caryn Collins was. And if they didn't have an answer he liked, then, whatever it took, one of them *would* talk.

CHAPTER TWELVE

It had taken forty minutes from the time they had left the co-op, but finally the computer indicated they had arrived near the rear perimeter of Lilly Arthur's farm. Carl turned the Cherokee onto a narrow dirt road that led off through a grassy field. At best, the road qualified as a tractor trail—two packed-dirt ruts with grass growing along either side and between the ruts. The road twisted and wove its way through the tall wild grass. It ended a third of a mile off the main country road after crossing three knolls and a small wet-weather creek. From all available intelligence, Lilly Arthur's homestead was a half mile due south. But from the end of the road, the warriors could see nothing but another grassy knoll and more tall grass.

Carl stopped the Jeep and shut the engine off. Both highway warriors climbed from the customized war machine without speaking. They went to the rear and opened the tailgate, gathered their equipment, and secured everything in place with the precision of a top-notch surgical team before major surgery. Both men carried silenced 9-mm Uzi submachine guns, a Beretta 92-SBF 9-mm automatic in a leg holster, and a Smith & Wesson 5096 9-mm stainless-steel automatic in a hip holster. On their waists, they secured their Uncle Mike's nylon-web utility belts with musette pack, spare magazine pouches, and Parker-Imai K-632 survival knife. When the weapons were loaded, checked, and secured, each warrior slid the belt clip of an Icom IC-U16 UHF hand-held transceiver on the belt.

The utility pockets of their black battle-dress utilities

bulged with spare magazines for the weapons. Four hand grenades dangled from nylon straps across their chests. Carl carried the Tasco 8 x 50 rubber armored binoculars; Marc strung a pair of infrared night field glasses across his shoulder just in case the mission went longer than planned.

"You ready?" Carl asked.

"Just a sec." Marc reached into the storage box in the rear of the Jeep and came out with a spray can of odorless insect repellent. "Better use some of this in all that tall grass. It's a bad year for ticks. The last thing we need is Rocky Mountain Spotted Fever or lyme disease. Call it our ounce of prevention." He sprayed the lower portion of his BDUs, then the top of his body.

Carl took the can when Marc was finished and did exactly as Marc had done. "That'd be our luck, wouldn't it?"

"What's that?"

"With the hells we've been through, it'd be our luck to die from some damned tick bite."

Marc laughed and checked the audio level on the Icom transceiver. "Stranger things have happened. It pays to be prepared. Let's do it."

"Ready when you are, bro."

The warriors left the Jeep and waded through the chest-high wild grass until they reached the top of the first grassy knoll fifty yards away. When they approached the knoll, they dropped low to ensure they weren't detected by a lookout.

They stopped atop the knoll and looked at the breathtaking beauty of the picturesque farm lying three hundred yards below them. Carl scanned the house and the barn with the binoculars. "Looks mighty quiet down there, Colonel."

"Yeah, but not for long. Here comes a blue van into the driveway over by the road."

Carl jerked the binoculars back to his face and found the van. He focused on it as it twisted up the long gravel lane. "A man and a woman, best I can tell. It's a Dodge."

Marc smiled, and then his face hardened. "Bingo. I just love the advantages of modern technology. Let's go collect society's debt."

The warriors moved stealthily through the tall grass, increasingly on the lookout for trip wires or booby traps. It wasn't likely the scumbags had taken the time to prepare any welcoming devices, but it paid to be cautious.

The unexpected sound of a car engine stopped both warriors in their tracks. The car seemed to appear from out of nowhere, but it took only a second for Marc and Carl to realize it had been in front of the barn all along. More shocking than the sound of the engine and the appearance of the car itself was the fact that it was a sheriff's patrol car.

The highway warriors held their breath and watched. The driver of the car drove off through the fields on another farm trail that led west, away from the farm. In less than a minute, the patrol car vanished behind tall grass, and the sound faded away.

"What do you make of that?" Carl asked softly.

Marc shook his head. "Don't know. Something isn't right. What're your thoughts?"

Carl's lips barely moved. His voice was just above a whisper, and his eyes scanned every object in the farmyard. "Could be they hid well, and the sheriff just drove away. Then again, it's possible the scumbags got the drop on them and iced 'em. Hard to say. What do you want to do—sit awhile or go on in?"

"Let's work our way to the barn and be positive of what we have here. The last thing we need is a screwup."

"Affirmative on that, Colonel."

Marc kept his eyes on the farmhouse and spoke in a whisper. "Once we've secured the barn, we can split up and get ready to move in. I want to be damned sure before we go rushing into that farmhouse. We've got to watch and be sure that patrol car doesn't come popping back over the knoll. If the escapees and Collins's people are in there, the cops appearing at the wrong time could cause a bloodbath."

"If the information was right and this Hartley character wants to finish his work, there may have already been a bloodbath."

Marc maintained the whisper. "Let's get to that barn and see if any answers are in there."

Both men moved at the same time and threaded their way through the grass. In less than five minutes, they were at the back of the barn beside a walk-through door.

Marc was the first to peek through the cracks in the weathered boards, and what he saw made him smile. He whispered very softly to Carl, "This is it."

They had started through the door when they heard an unusual sound from inside the barn. Marc flipped the safety off on the silenced Uzi and moved slowly, cautiously, through the door in a low crouch.

The sound came again. Voices. They were low, but it sounded like two people talking. The sound was muffled, but then the door to one of the show buses opened.

Marc motioned to Carl to go to the right, around the eighteen-wheelers and the second bus. Marc went left, along the driver's side of the bus where the voices had come from. He moved slowly, staying low to the ground in a waddling motion that resembled a duckwalk. He held the Uzi against his chest, his finger resting on the trigger. Each breath he drew was slow and methodical.

There was movement on the bus now, as if someone were walking. Marc worked his way to the front of the giant vehicle, then slid stealthily around the front bumper until he was within a few steps of the open door of the bus. He took a deep breath, looked to his left for Carl, and listened.

Carl was already in position. He had worked his way around Caryn Collins's vehicles and was squatting at the front of an eighteen-wheeler. He gave the hand sign, using a sequence he and Marc had worked out years before indicating he would wait for Marc to move in and then come in as backup.

Marc let his breath out and took another deep one. His professional skills were at their height, his senses at full alert. He came up from the crouch, his finger cradling the Uzi's trigger. In two steps, he cleared the open bus door and made his first giant lunge onto the steps of the bus. His face was hard, mean, and filled with a look that meant death to anyone in his way. The muzzle of the Uzi stopped on two men in the front of the bus. Marc spoke firmly, his voice filled with authority. "Don't even breathe. Keep your hands where I can see them. Lay that pistol down nice and slow. Now, who the hell are you?"

Dennis Goodman couldn't speak because he knew he was dead. Wilbur's face turned ghostly white, and his mouth dropped open at the sight of the hard-looking man holding the submachine gun. Finally, Goodman managed some words. "Who are *you*?"

"Oh, no. I'm asking the questions. You're giving the answers. Who are you, and where are the others?"

Goodman was stuttering. Between the pain and fear, it was very difficult for him to speak. "I'm Dennis Goodman. I . . . work for—for Caryn Collins. Are you g-going to kill us?"

"That's up to you. Where's Caryn Collins?"

"Caryn? You mean you're not one of them?"

"Who is 'them'?"

Goodman strained to make the words come. "The—the people who k-kidnapped us."

Marc let the Uzi drop. "I'm here to get you out. What happened to you, and who is this man?"

Goodman felt a massive relief. "This is Wilbur Matthews. He owns the farm that adjoins this place. He happened on me 'cause he hadn't heard anything from the old woman who owns this place. God, am I glad to see you. How did you find us?"

"It's a very long story, and I'm not sure you'd believe it if I told you. What happened to you? You're bleeding quite a bit."

"I made a run for it. Then some deputy sheriff shot me. Those bastards in the house killed him and his partner. I heard the sheriff's car drive to the front of the barn a few minutes ago. They picked up the deputy's body and drove away. Can you get us out of here?"

Marc smiled. "That's my specialty."

Goodman also forced a smile. "Are you, uh, alone?"

A voice came from behind Marc at the doorway. "No, he's not alone. I'm right behind him. Me and this gun. Now, cowboy, lay that Uzi down real carefully and tell me who the hell you are before my finger starts to itch more than I can control. Get cute, and I'll splatter you all over the inside of this nice bus."

———

There had been several times in the preceding hours that Richie Halloway wondered if Cliff Scott and Amy would return. He had chastised himself for giving Scott so much cash and such a grand opportunity to leave and never look back. He had chosen Cliff Scott for the escape because he trusted him and Amy represented the perfect way to leave the prison without arousing suspicion. Cliff Scott was loyal to the effort; not only the escape, but the preplanned extortion by way of kidnapping. But even for hard-core types, loyalty had a mysterious way of vanishing when survival became the paramount issue. And from the very instant the prison-made knives spilled the first drop of guard's blood, survival was the only issue.

When Richie saw the dark blue van start up the long, winding lane to the old farmhouse, a broad smile crossed his face. The sight of the van, the very fact that it was there, proved Scott's loyalty. It also proved that Richie was a pretty fair judge of character. More than anything else, it was a massive relief. An additional burden Richie didn't need was immediately lifted from his shoulders.

Richie yelled to Lionel Lewis that Scott had returned. He hit the porch running for the second time in less than an hour. The shotgun that had become his constant companion dangled in his right hand. He met Scott with a welcome that would have, under different circumstances, been adequate for the homecoming of a long-lost relative.

Ray Hartley hadn't been that excited. He preferred to get the patrol car and the bodies away from the farm rather than spend valuable time socializing. Before he started the gruesome chore of cleaning up the remains of dead cops and heroic captives, Hartley had seen to his own obsession—Lilly Arthur. He forcibly escorted the frail old woman back to the bedroom on the second floor and locked her inside. From the utterances she kept repeating, Hartley decided, the excitement had been too much for her. She had obviously lost whatever mind she had left. Hartley figured she had gone over the edge into psychological oblivion, but he hadn't changed his mind about killing the old bitch. And if she had gone over the edge, then so much the better. It would add to her emotional torment before he finished the murder he had started nine years earlier. This time, he would look her in the eyes, just as he'd done with old Jesse in the front yard. And this time, he'd be damned sure she didn't come back to testify against him. Ever.

Hartley had completed the chore of loading the bodies by himself. And although Sheriff Jesse Thomas had little left of either face or head, it gave Ray a great sense of pride to heave the body of the man, who had brutally clamped the handcuffs around his wrists nine years before, into the car. He had given the son of a bitch just what he deserved—a load of 00-buckshot in the face. His only regret was that he hadn't put a .30-30 slug through the lawman bastard's chest when he had led the posse to bring him out of the hills. Killing Jesse Thomas had been a bonus, and the great part was that no one would ever find a body to bury. And once Cliff Scott got the spray-paint rig set up and they painted one of the eighteen-wheelers, no one would ever find Ray Hartley to clamp another pair of handcuffs around his wrists. And no judge would ever send him behind the walls of hell for another murder. Why? Because once the root of his obsession was dead, Ray Hartley had nothing else to live for.

Halloway, Scott, and Markham stood at the back of the van now, inspecting the supplies purchased with money taken from Bernie Aldridge. Halloway was very pleased. "You did good work, guys. Where's the beer?"

Scott laughed. "We drank it all before we got back."

Halloway jumped back from the van. "You did what? I thought I told you not to—"

Scott interrupted. "Be cool, man, it's in the front behind the seats. We behaved well. Right, Amy?"

Amy hesitated, and her response was tinged with sarcasm. "Right, Cliff."

Scott laughed again. "Well, we almost behaved. There was one little loose end we tied up permanently."

Halloway got very excited. "What does that mean?"

"The straight shirt at the civic center. The one that saw us get on Collins's buses. Remember him?"

"Yeah. So?"

"So he could identify me and you. I went back and made damned sure he'd never testify against us."

"How?"

"I put a bullet through his forehead. He won't be tellin' anybody anything. Let's just say I sanitized our tracks."

"Damn, Cliff, not good. The cops, man. What if he'd already talked?"

"No sweat, he hadn't, but he was sure thinkin' about it. He saw our pictures on TV. We're stars, man. The funny thing is, without my beard, nobody gave me a second glance the whole time we were in town. People are dumb, you know that, Rich?"

"Wow, Cliff. I wish you hadn't done that. That just gives 'em something else to tie in to us."

Scott was taking it all lightheartedly. "Not to worry, man. I made it look like a robbery attempt. You know, I tossed shit around and kinda wrecked the place. No way anybody will ever pin that one on us."

"Damn! Well, it's done now. Let's get this stuff unloaded."

"Bullshit! We've done our part. Get some of them roadies in the back room to unload. They're paid to do heavy work."

"Good idea. Lionel could use a little break anyway. We had a few problems ourselves while you were gone. I'll tell you about it in a little while. I'll go get some cheap labor and be right back."

Halloway turned and walked toward the front porch. Scott yelled at him. "Hey, Rich, where's Ray?"

Halloway stopped and turned to face Scott. "He's over on the west side of the farm. He'll be back in a little while. There was something he had to take care of."

A puzzled look crossed Scott's face. It didn't make sense, but he let it ride and went back to arranging the boxes of food for unloading.

Amy moved in beside Cliff at the rear of the van. She tossed the bangs out of her eyes and leaned in close to Cliff. "I don't like it, Cliff. Something's wrong here. Let's split. We can get into Canada before anybody finds us. Let these guys take care of themselves. You've done your part and so have I. I don't care about Richie's money anymore. How 'bout it?"

Cliff was taken off-guard. "Why now, Amy? Why not when we were in town or before we came here?"

"I'm tellin' you, Cliff. I got a bad feeling about this. Something's wrong. I feel like it's all gettin' ready to crash around us."

Cliff sat on the edge on the van floor between the open doors. He looked at Amy for a moment, his face showing disbelief and frustration. "I don't understand. What could be wrong? We're out here in the middle of nowhere. Nobody but us and the people we got inside have the slightest idea where we are. I'm not so sure we could do any better in Canada."

Amy's pretty face filled with a look of uncertain fear. "Cliff, I'm tellin' you. Call it woman's intuition, but I got a feelin' that something very bad is about to happen. I think we need to get this stuff out of the van and leave this place. We'll do better on our own."

"Amy, we got all the time in the world. We took the tape to the radio station just like Rich wanted us too. In a few days at the most, we'll have more money than any of us will ever need. Now we owe it to ourselves and to Richie to hang in there. We quit now, and we'll never get out of this country alive—any of us."

Amy was getting angrier by the minute. Her voice was filled with anger and disgust. She looked into Cliff's eyes, her eyes scolding him. "Cliff, you're my brother, and I love you for whatever you are, but you're being stupid, really stupid. What do you think you're going to do with all those people inside? You go back to a civic center and kill one man who saw you. That made you kill the girl who saw you kill him. And those people . . . Caryn Collins . . . what are we gonna do, kill all of them? They saw us. They know us. They've lived with us for days. you think they're gonna just pay a bunch of money to Richie and then forget the whole thing ever happened? That's insane. They'll never stop looking for us. Maybe now we at least have a chance to put all this shit behind us and live a new life somewhere."

Scott didn't know what to say. He just sat there. Seconds passed, and then he looked back at Amy. "I think it would be a mistake to leave. You wanna go, then go. I won't stop you. I'm staying. I ain't goin' back to the joint. No way. I'll never go back to the joint. And you're in this up over your ass. They catch us, you're goin' down for murder, same as the rest of us. You better think about that. You want to spend the rest of your life in prison? Or worse, you want to fry in the chair?"

Amy's jaw sank, and her face filled with sadness. "How'd we ever get this way, Cliff? How?"

Cliff started to answer, then heard the sound of the door opening on the front porch. He spun around and looked in that direction. Richie Halloway came out of the door behind three men from Caryn Collins's entourage. He held his shotgun at hip level, pointed at the three men. They walked in a straight line to the van and stopped in front of Scott and Amy.

Halloway issued the orders. "Get this food and stuff moved into the house. Cliff, get your shotgun and watch 'em from out here. I'll stand guard in the house. Anybody tries anything cute, blow his ass away. You guys hear that?"

All three men nodded.

"Okay, get with it."

Amy moved to the side of the van, out of the way, while Cliff went to retrieve his shotgun from behind the front seat. Richie moved back a few steps and held the shotgun on the men. In seconds, Cliff returned with the sawed-off shotgun. He stood to the side where he could have a clear shot. Each of the men gathered a load of groceries and walked toward the house. Halloway followed.

It took ten minutes to unload all the food supplies. The last things to be unloaded were the air compressor and paint for the spray gun. Cliff Scott stopped the men when they started to remove the air compressor. "Hold it. Don't unload that. Amy, go tell Rich to come out here."

Amy ran into the house. A minute later, Halloway appeared. "Yeah, Cliff?"

Cliff pointed to the air compressor. "Let's just take this to the barn. No need unloading it here when we can do it there. That's where we're gonna use it."

Richie nodded his head in agreement. "Good idea. Take it to the barn."

CHAPTER THIRTEEN

Carl had heard the man the instant he came into the barn through the back door. Then he had watched the guy slip along the side of the bus. He knew Marc couldn't hear him. There was no way to let Marc know. Marc stood inside the bus with his back to the eighteen-wheeler. He thought about keying his transmitter, but he decided that might spook the approaching gunman.

Carl waited and crawled under the front of the eighteen-wheeler before he made his move. He let the guy move into the bus and when he heard him give orders to Marc, Carl slipped from beneath the rig and moved carefully toward the man with the gun. If he took him alive, he could get some answers.

In a situation where any sound, any detected movement, could mean a deadly betrayal, Carl knew there was no margin for error, exactly the kind of situation Carl knew he was in now. He moved methodically and very, very cautiously as he approached the man holding the gun at Marc's back. He came out from under the eighteen-wheel rig on his hands and knees. His breathing was slow and deliberate, just like every step he took. In a low crunch now, he moved to the bus. The Uzi sat perched on his hip, hugged in close to his body. His finger rested on the trigger, ready to cause 9-mm instant death to spit from the Uzi's muzzle. Three steps to go now. The man with the gun wasn't sure what he was going to do next, but Carl was. Two steps. One.

The man with the gun pointed at Marc twitched nervously for an instant when Carl's cold, authoritative voice came from behind him. "Red, you lose. Now, if you

123

don't want your ass shredded like a pile of confetti, lay those weapons on the floor, very carefully. You mess up or try to be a hero, and I'm going to give you a brand-new asshole. Do it!"

The gunman leaned over and gently placed his weapons on the floor. He raised up with a disgusted look on his face. "Who the hell *are* you guys?"

Marc turned around and looked the man in the eyes. The muzzle of his Uzi aimed directly at the guy's midsection. "Oh, no. You don't understand. We ask the questions. You give the answers. Because we got the guns. Who the hell are *you*?"

The man took a deep breath and exhaled. He rubbed his face with his right hand. "Name's O'Connall. Roy O'Connall. I'm a private investigator from St. Louis."

The response hit Marc like a ton of bricks crashing into his head. O'Connall. St. Louis. "O'Connall as in Shannon O'Connall?"

"Unfortunately, yes. He's my brother, but don't hold that against me."

"Why are you here?"

"I'm on a case. And don't tell me, let me guess. You're just a couple of truck drivers who took a wrong turn. Am I right?"

Marc forced a grin. "I guess you could say that. I'll ask just once more: Why are you here?"

"I told you already. I'm on a case."

Carl's voice came from behind O'Connall again. "The man likes details. Considering the position you're in right now, I suggest you give him some real quick."

"Persuasive, aren't you? I'm working for Interstate Leasing Services. They own these buses. Since Miss Collins disappeared, they wanted to find their property, so it could be protected. If Caryn Collins happened to be included in the package, so much the better."

Marc forced another smile. "Right. Your brother hired you?"

"That's right. Who *are* you guys? I mean, you're running around in an eighteen-wheeler, and then you pop up looking like a couple of gung-ho commandos. What the hell is this?"

Marc spoke in a low, firm voice. "Business. We're here to protect our interests."

"What interests?"

"These eighteen-wheel rigs belong to Leeco Freight Lines. Collins leases them. We wanted to be sure they weren't in any danger. We just happened to be in the general area and thought we'd drop in and check on 'em. How'd you find this place?"

"Right, business. If you guys are everyday truck drivers, I'm a Mongolian aviator. I found this place because I'm good at what I do. Why?"

Carl chuckled. "I'll tell you why. My finger's gettin' real itchy on this trigger, that's why."

"Okay, okay. Looks like you guys are holdin' all the winning cards. I got on the trail of these creeps at the civic center in North Platte. I went there for a meeting with the director. When I got there, one of these shitbags had just left. He iced the manager because the guy had seen him getting on Caryn Collins's bus the night she was abducted. I been following the clown all day long. He brought me here, but he doesn't know that."

"Who?"

"Come on, guys, don't play dumb, because obviously you ain't. The scumbag's name is Cliff Scott. I ID'd the guy at a store in North Platte. He's traveling with some broad in a blue Dodge van. He and the rest of these creeps are prison escapees from the Nebraska state pen. I imagine you already knew that."

Marc nodded his head. "You're right so far. Keep talking."

"Hey, who are *these* people?" O'Connall pointed to Goodman and Matthews.

Marc gestured with his left hand, his right hand on the Uzi. "The one sitting down is Dennis Goodman. He works for Caryn Collins. This is Wilbur Matthews. He owns the farm that adjoins this one, behind us to the north. We just met before you came along. I got one question, O'Connall: If Scott killed the manager at the civic center, then how did you know he had seen Scott getting on the bus with Collins?"

"He didn't finish his work. He wounded the manager's secretary. She was still alive when I got there. She was hurt bad, but she managed to tell me everything that happened before she lost it. She knew about the blue van. When I left, I caught sight of the van and then lost it. It took awhile, but I caught up with 'em again and made the positive ID. So here I am. What next?"

Marc let the muzzle of the Uzi drop toward the floor. He stepped over to Dennis Goodman. "Since you're here, O'Connall, we've got a lot to do if we're going to get those people out of that house. You can stay if you want, or you can leave. If you stay, we call the shots, and you do what we tell you. Is that clear?"

"No problem."

Marc leaned over and checked Dennis Goodman's wounds. The bandages were seeping blood. Goodman was wide-eyed at the turn of events, but he didn't say anything.

Marc stood and looked at Carl who still remained on the bottom step of the bus. "Okay, first we've got to get this man proper medical attention. He's still bleeding, and he's going into shock. We need a Life Flight helicopter or a Medevac unit here, and we need it as soon as we can get it."

O'Connall almost laughed. "What are you gonna do, go up to the house and ask to use the telephone?"

Marc grinned. "Technology, my friend, technology." He lifted the Icom from his belt and pressed the buttons to change the channel. When the one he wanted appeared, he pressed another numerical sequence to activate the minirepeater in the Cherokee just over the hill behind the barn. The repeater linked into the Icom IC-V100 transceiver. When he was satisfied with the link, he entered another numerical sequence that linked the V100 into the Defense Department's nationwide repeater system through the ComSat-D orbiting satellite high above Earth. The link would take him directly to Brittin Crain at FBI headquarters in Washington or to the control operator at Delta Force Command deep underground in the Pentagon. When ComSat-D was engaged, Marc pressed the transmit switch once and listened to the squelch tails. Then he lifted the transceiver to his face and pressed the transmit switch. "Barnburner, this is Pathfinder. Do you copy? Over."

No answer. Roy O'Connall stood with his mouth almost open, but he didn't say anything.

Marc made the call again. "Barnburner, this is Pathfinder. You read me? Over."

A voice foreign to Marc crackled over the Icom's speaker. "Roger, Pathfinder, this is Barnburner at DFC. Go ahead with your traffic. Over."

"Roger, Barnburner. I need a link to Mr. Crain immediately. Priority traffic. Over."

"Roger, Pathfinder. Stand by."

Several seconds passed, and then another voice crackled through the speaker, slow with a deep southern drawl. "Pathfinder, this is Barnburner. Over."

"Barnburner, we have reached the target. Repeat, we have reached the target. We have not encountered the objective, but they are here. Call off all incoming. Repeat, call off all incoming. We want to handle this one by ourselves. Over."

"Roger."

Marc pressed the transmit switch again. "Barnburner, we have wounded here. We need a Life Flight helicopter or a Medevac unit immediately. Send them to the coordinates you gave us earlier. Have the pilot approach from the north and stay clear of the target zone. Instruct him not to come near here. We'll evacuate the wounded and meet him a mile north of the exact coordinates. Tell him to come in low and be sure he understands to come in only from the north. Over."

"Roger, Pathfinder. We're looking as we speak. Have you one from somewhere in a minute. What's the scoop? Over."

"We're not sure. We have located the escapees, and we have them under observation. We also have the objective under surveillance. We're going to evacuate this wounded man and then rethink our plan. We'll probably wait and come in during the night. If we're cautious, we can execute the surgical extraction at that time without too much risk of lost lives. Over."

Roy O'Connall was trying to absorb it all. He looked very puzzled when he spoke. "Code names on radios, helicopters, surgical extractions. Who the hell *are* you guys?"

Marc ignored him and listened to Brittin's voice on the radio.

Carl's spoke excitedly, and that changed Marc's attention. "I heard something. Be quiet." Carl ran to the front of the barn and peeped between the cracks in the weathered wood. He ran back to the bus. "We gotta get out of here. The van's coming across the yard, and it's headed this way. We don't need a confrontation now."

Marc was stern. "Okay, O'Connall. You take Wilbur and get out of here. Go straight out the back and through the tall grass. Meet on the other side of the knoll. You'll see the Jeep Cherokee there. I'll take Goodman. Carl, you know what to do."

Carl acknowledged. "Got it, Colonel."

O'Connall draped the Mini-14 over his shoulder on its sling. He took Wilbur by the arm and led him from the bus. He walked along side of the bus until he reached the back of the barn. As he walked, he mumbled aloud, "Truck drivers, my ass."

Marc leaned over and lifted Dennis Goodman from his seat. He threw him over his shoulder in a modified fireman's carry. "Dennis, sorry for the quality of the ride, but it's the best I can do under the circumstances. Hang tight."

Goodman managed a painfilled reply. "I'm hangin', man. Thanks."

Carl went back to the front of the barn and watched. The van was almost there now. He looked back at Marc just in time to see him disappear through the back door. Carl quickly ran to the bus and closed the door. That finished, he made a dead run for the back door. Just as he closed the back door, the front door squeaked open. He made a mad dive for the tall grass, rolled over, and fell prone, the Uzi pointed at the back door. And then he heard the voices.

Mike Coble was fighting the odds, clinging desperately to life. His neck was cut badly, but the knife's blade had severed mostly muscle tissue and missed the carotid artery. The bleeding from severed veins had slowed, and at least his esophagus wasn't penetrated. That was probably the only reason he was still alive.

Caryn Collins knelt beside the big roadie on the floor, Bernie Aldridge at her side, comforting her. Coble had slipped into the darkness of unconsciousness almost instantly after the wounds were inflicted. At first, when he had hit the floor and Collins reached him, she thought he was dead. Closer examination revealed a pulse and unsteady but vital breathing.

Collins looked around the room at the dejected faces of those remaining. Dennis Goodman was gone, probably dead. Bernie Aldridge had been little comfort. Caryn wondered if perhaps his only interest in life was money. Greed, pure and simple. He had expressed no hostility, no shock, when the shots were fired inside the room. For the first time in her professional career, Caryn thought she saw the real Bernie Aldridge, and what she saw made her sick to her stomach. She decided that unless he made some effort to gain their freedom, unless he acted like a man instead of a whipped pup, she would fire him the minute she walked away from this nightmare.

She looked at Aldridge and tried not to let her feelings show. She spoke to him in a low whisper. "Bernie, you've got to do something to get us out of here. The longer we stay, the more likely they'll kill us. We've been here for days. If we don't find out what these people *really* want, we're going to die right here on this farm."

Aldridge looked shocked at the suggestion that it was his responsibility to get them out. "What do you expect *me* to do, Caryn? They've got the guns. They've got the money from the concessions. What can I give them?"

"I don't know, Bernie. If I knew, I wouldn't need you to find out, would I?"

Aldridge tried to console her. "Look, I know this is hard on you. It's hard on all of us. I wish you wouldn't be so headstrong and testy. I want out of here just as much as you do. I think we need to remain calm. The time will come when we can strike. We'll know it when it comes."

"Right, Bernie. How are you going to know it? Maybe by the blood running down our faces, you chickenshit wimp! You've really disappointed me. I thought you were a bigger man than this."

"Caryn, darling. I wish you wouldn't use language like that, even in private. You're going to mess up one of these days, and then it'll be on the cover of every music magazine in the country."

"Dammit, Bernie, I'd rather it be my foul mouth than pictures of my funeral. If you're too damned scared to talk to these assholes, then I will. I'll get us out of here if I have to pay these people all the money we *both* have."

"Caryn, calm down. Okay, I'll talk to them. This Richie Halloway is the one in charge. He's the one we need to see."

"You know something you aren't telling me, don't you, Bernie?"

Aldridge felt the blood rise to his face. He knew he couldn't hide it any longer. "Yes, Caryn, I do."

"Well, are you gonna tell me or keep it to yourself forever?"

Bernie took a deep breath and looked Collins directly in the eyes. "I know what this is all about, Caryn."

"I'm listening."

"It's about your current single."

"Okay, so what? Halloway doesn't like it, or what?"

"Quite the contrary. He loves it. You see, over a year ago, I received a tape in the mail. You know I don't usually listen to those things when they come in without a solicitation, but this one had a letter with it. I read the letter and decided to put the tape on and give it an honest listen. I'm glad I did. The song was written by Richie Halloway, and the letter said he was serving a life sentence in prison. As soon as I heard the song, I knew it'd be a smash—given the right production, of course."

Caryn was listening intently, the fire building inside her. "Of course, Mr. Perfect Production Man. Go on."

"It took me two weeks to contact Halloway. I told him

I would have you record the song if he would consent to you and me splitting the publishing rights to it. He agreed over the telephone, and I mailed him a contract. That satisfied him. When I received the signed contract back from him, I never signed it. As a matter of fact, I tore it up and trashed it. I figured he was serving life in prison—he sure as hell couldn't do much, so I played the song for you after I had another demo tape cut on it. We changed a few words here and there, and then I put your name and mine on it."

Caryn was livid now, but she knew she had to keep her cool or attract Lionel Lewis's attention, even through the fog of his pain. "You *stole* the damned song, Bernie? You told me you wrote it and you wanted to split it with me. You lying, thieving son of a bitch. How many others, Bernie? How many of my other records have been stolen songs?"

Aldridge knew he had a problem. "Caryn, please listen to me. This is the only one. I swear it. Look what this song has done for you. You've got a number-one record out of it. You'll make thousands upon thousands of dollars from it in airplay royalties alone. That doesn't even consider the mechanicals or TV. This guy was a dirtbag. I never thought he could get out of a maximum-security prison."

"Shit! Bernie, what if the guy had just decided to sue us? What then?"

"Get off it, Caryn. What court would believe a convicted murderer over a national superstar? Get real."

"It's stealin', Bernie. There's just no other way to put it. I think we need to come clean with the story in public and give this man what he rightfully deserves. I think you need to make the first public admission. Furthermore, I believe Richie Halloway is entitled to every dime this song ever earns and I think you, Bernie Aldridge, are an underhanded sack of shit!"

"Caryn, listen to reason. They're gonna catch this guy and when they do, his ass is goin' back in the slammer for the rest of his life. They'll probably cook him medium-rare on the hot seat. What's he gonna need with money?"

"You're lower than I thought, Bernie. You're trash.

I'm going to talk to Richie Halloway. I'm going to tell him that I just this minute learned the truth about the song and about you. I'm also going to tell him that he is entitled to every red cent this song makes, for as long as it makes it. I don't care if he goes to Antarctica and wants his money sent to a Swiss bank account. He's going to get every penny of it. And when this is over, Bernie, you're going to get what you deserve too."

Aldridge felt the blood that had flooded his head earlier rush to his feet, and he felt faint. He knew he was pale now. He knew he had been discovered, and that meant a great many problems. Too many. "Caryn, please listen to reason. These people have seen us, and we have seen them. I don't care what you give them. Do you really think they're going to let us leave this farm alive when we can identify them? Think about it."

Collins smiled. "Okay, Bernie, I thought about it." She turned away from Aldridge and looked at Lionel Lewis. "Lionel."

Lewis jerked alert. "Yeah, Mama? Whatta you want?"

"I want to see Richie Halloway. I think he and I can reach an equitable business agreement."

CHAPTER FOURTEEN

Marc ran as fast as he could. Breathing came hard now, and he knew he had to keep moving. The tall wild grass provided some cover, but in order to utilize it effectively, he had to stay low, in a crouch. The added weight of Dennis Goodman across his shoulders slowed his run and increased the pain.

Roy O'Connall was ahead of him. He had managed to make Wilbur Matthews move faster than Marc had thought the old man could. O'Connall and Matthews had disappeared over the crest of the grassy knoll before Marc reached the halfway point.

Carl maintained his position outside of the barn, prone in the tall grass. His right index finger cradled the silenced Uzi's trigger and he waited. He knew there was no use to try to call Marc on the Icom. Marc had switched from the simplex frequency they normally used for close-range work, and Carl knew the big highway warrior hadn't had an opportunity to change back. To move his own radio to the ComSat-D link frequency would not be prudent. Although the frequency and all transmissions were digitally encoded and decoded, to have their current dilemma transmitted around the United States wouldn't be good business. Carl decided to play it by ear. He could hear the voices inside the barn—three people: two men and one woman. He fixed his eyes on the back of the old weather-beaten barn and waited.

Marc was nearing the top of the knoll. On the other side would be relative safety. He could then stand and relieve his lower back and legs of Dennis Goodman's weight. Somewhere during the run, he had felt Goodman's body go completely limp; either the run had caused him to pass into unconsciousness, or he was dead. When he reached the other side of the hill, Marc would stop and find out. Right now, there wasn't time.

Roy O'Connall reached the Jeep Cherokee first. He and Wilbur Matthews waited for Marc. Finally, he saw the highway warrior pop over the top of the hill. "Wilbur, I hate to run, but I'm gonna see if I can help the big guy out."

Wilbur answered without any hesitation. "I ain't goin' nowhere, young feller. I ain't seen this much excitement in forty years. I'll be right here."

O'Connall took off running. The big warrior had stopped to rest. He had laid Goodman on the ground, and he checked for a pulse when O'Connall stopped beside him. "Is he still alive?"

Marc was breathing hard. His lungs burned, and his legs throbbed. "Yeah, barely. All that jostling and bumping didn't do him any good."

O'Connall knelt down beside Goodman. "Okay, let's get him down to the Jeep. We can get him to Wilbur's pickup from there. How 'bout I take a turn?"

Marc nodded as he struggled to breathe. "Yeah . . . I won't . . . argue with you there. This old boy hasn't missed any meals lately . . . he's heavy. Sure you can handle him?"

O'Connall flexed his arms and reached for Goodman. "Hey, I'll give it the old college try. I've always been pretty good at the long haul."

Marc was still getting his breath. "Yeah, well, it's . . . it's sure a long one up that hill. That sucker didn't look that steep when I started up it . . . help you get him on your shoulders."

"No, you rest. I can handle it. Honest."

"It's your back. Whatever you say."

Roy grabbed Dennis Goodman by the arms and legs, picked him up, and laid him across his shoulders. Without another word, he walked toward the Jeep.

Marc watched in disbelief. He stood and quickly caught up with O'Connall. "You're pretty stout for a man your size. You lift weights?"

"I used to. Haven't done it in years. I miss it, too. Think Goodman will make it?"

"If the Medevac unit gets here, he's got a damned good chance. If it doesn't, well..."

"Maybe this ain't the time, but I didn't catch your name."

"Could be because I didn't throw it out. Marc. Marc Lee."

"As in Leeco?"

"That's right. It's my father's company."

"Yeah, I know all about it. A lot of talk about all that mess in Dallas a while back. Everybody in the trucking industry knew about it. Some folks think you're a hero."

Marc was surprised by O'Connall's remark. "I just did what had to be done. Nothing more, nothing less."

"I can understand that. I would have probably done the same thing myself. I guess the other guy is Carl Browne. Am I right?"

"Yeah, that's right."

"I see. I knew you guys weren't just everyday truck drivers."

"That's what we are, truck drivers. We just happened to have had a bit of intensive training along the way. Got a few other specialities besides rollin' eighteen wheels."

"*Quite* a few from what I hear."

They reached the Jeep, and O'Connall waited while Marc retrieved his set of keys from his pants pocket and deactivated the digital alarm system. Once the Jeep was unlocked, O'Connall laid Dennis Goodman's limp body into the front passenger seat and snapped the seat belt around him. He scanned the electronics console, then looked at Marc. "You're a truck driver and this is a factory Jeep, right?"

Marc grinned. "Now you're gettin' the hang of it. You may have possibilities if you keep learnin' that fast." Marc handed the Jeep keys to O'Connall. "Here, you take Wilbur home and unload Goodman. They can wait there for the chopper. And, Wilbur, don't call the police or anybody else. We have everything under control. Deal?"

Wilbur smiled. "Yes, sir. Anything you say. I'll wait for that there whirlybird to come get him."

"Good. Roy, I'll be hangin' around lookin' for scumbags when you get back. Be careful."

O'Connall shrugged his shoulders. "I won't be long. Save a couple for me, will you?"

Marc nodded. "You got it."

O'Connall entered the driver's seat while Wilbur climbed into the back of the Cherokee. Roy started the engine, dropped the Cherokee into gear, and turned through the tall grass.

Marc backed away and then had an afterthought. He waved for O'Connall to stop. "Hey, one thing I forgot."

"What's that?"

"I wouldn't push any unfamiliar buttons while you're in there. Anything might happen . . . if you catch my drift."

O'Connall managed a short laugh. "Yeah, big guy, I catch it." Roy rolled the window up and drove away.

Marc walked back through the grass to the top of the knoll. He squatted low and scanned the peaceful-looking farm below. There was an air of tranquillity about the place, but Marc knew that initial impression was a mask of deception. In the midst of American heartland tranquillity lurked the menace of death—quietly and cunningly. But there was one thing he knew that the inhabitants of the serene farm didn't: Although the prison escapees were the darkness of death incarnate, another dark cloud loomed above them—the permanent sword of final justice in the shape of two highway warriors. And when the lightning swath of that mighty sword struck with a vengeance, there could be no escape for the evil.

Marc settled down on one knee and looked for Carl. He couldn't see him, but he knew his partner in the never-ending war on crime was there somewhere. He laid out a plan. The El Salvador scheme would work, and the addition of Roy O'Connall to the assault team made the odds tip just a little further in favor of justice. Despite their initial dislike for each other, Marc thought the red-headed private eye just might be real good people. The shroud of darkness that would soon approach from the east would tell that. If O'Connall carried his weight and lived through the night, there was a chance he might be all right.

The tall wild grass parted in his wake as Marc moved

with the cunning of a cat toward the barn and Carl Browne. He occasionally glanced toward the western sky; it reminded him of Dallas. The long, jagged fingers of red that bounced off the scattered clouds from the dying rays of sunlight made him think of his father and the walks they sometimes took over their Texas ranch when he was a child. That was all gone forever now. Then the streaky red clouds took on the shape of the blood he had seen flow down the side of his father's face because of the freelance brutality of dirtbags.

If Marc ever had any doubts about the mission he and Carl had undertaken, they all dissipated when he thought of what criminal scum did to innocent human lives. The traumatic shock wave took an invisible toll far beyond the victim. Marc paused and stared at the sky as the sun settled slowly over the western horizon. When darkness finally smothered this humble Nebraska farm, three angels of retribution for the evils perpetrated against innocents would descend into the belly of the beast. And if they couldn't tame the unruly creature, they would smite him.

———

The table in the center of the kitchen was made of hand-hewn oak. Lilly Arthur's father had made it in the 1920s. Until the death of her family, Lilly had served more meals on the old rustic table than she could have counted. But now there was a new purpose for the oak antique. Caryn Collins sat with her elbows propped on it, her hands folded beneath her chin. Across the table, Richie Halloway stared at her.

Caryn broke the ice. "Just what is it you really want, Richie?"

Halloway laughed, and his eyes spit fire. "I want the recognition I deserve for my creation. I want the money my creation has earned. I want safe passage out of this country. I also want three million dollars for what your manager's actions have made me do."

Collins was straight-faced and sincere. "Is that all?"

"Yes."

"If I can guarantee that and then some, will you and your friends allow us to leave here alive?"

"You're shittin' me, lady. I've laid awake at night in

that hell they call prison and dreamed of the day when I'd hear my song on the radio. *My song*. And when I finally get my chance, Bernie Aldridge tries to screw me out of it. Believe me, I'd like nothin' better than to kill that son of a bitch."

Caryn sympathized. "At this moment, that makes two of us. I've learned a lot about Bernie Aldridge in the last few days. He isn't the man I thought he was."

"Okay, so what are you tellin' me? You got three mill on the bus or what?"

"No, not hardly. If I do this, I'm going to need your cooperation. I will call my accountant in Nashville and have him wire three million dollars anywhere in the world you want it to go, no questions asked. Second, I will call the radio or television station of your choice and make a full disclosure of the facts surrounding this song. I knew nothing of it until Bernie admitted it to me just a few minutes ago. I mean that, Richie, from the bottom of my heart. I'm an honest person. I would never knowingly steal another person's song, no matter how great it was. Enough people have died over this already. Let's make an arrangement and get this ordeal over for both of us."

"Yeah, right. Get off it. I wasn't born yesterday. You make the telephone calls, and they trace 'em. We'll have cops swarmin' all over this place before we could hang up the telephone. I ain't stupid."

Caryn hadn't moved her hands or arms. She sat staring into Richie Halloway's eyes. "Richie, I'm so sorry for what has happened. I don't blame you for getting so upset. What happened to you wasn't right. I blame Bernie more than I blame you. I mean that. I think deep inside, there's a good Richie Halloway that's made some mistakes. I think this hard-core front you put up is just a device to hide all the hurt you've known. I don't think the Richie Halloway that wrote "Late Night Love" is the kind of man that could do some of the things you've done. I think you messed up somewhere, and nobody ever gave you a second chance to do things right."

Halloway mellowed. The woman had read him like the pages of an open book. "It's gone too far. I don't know any way to turn it back. God, I just don't know."

Caryn knew it was time to close the sale. "Richie, if I make those calls and then make a complete public disclosure of what really happened and how the song really came into being, will you let us go?"

"I can never stop running. All I can hope for is a chance to get into some other country where nobody knows me. It's a long way from Nebraska to the borders of the United States when every man with a gun and a badge is looking for you."

Caryn pressed harder. "You give me your word, and I'll make the call. I'm honest, and I'm a woman of my word. Banks won't be open until tomorrow, but I'll make the call tonight. The money can be transferred first thing tomorrow morning to anywhere you want it. Take one of the buses or your van. Take one of the eighteen-wheelers if you want that. But Richie, whatever you do, don't take any more lives. All the fame and money in the world isn't worth the value of one human life."

Halloway stiffened. "You ain't seen the world from where I have, lady. Money don't mean a thing when you got plenty of it. Freedom ain't important until you ain't free anymore. And love... yeah, love. Love makes nice songs for people to sing until nobody loves you anymore. But you wouldn't know any of that. You're Caryn Collins... superstar. Miss Wonderful. You don't know what it's like in my world. You couldn't."

Caryn dropped her hands. She reached across the table and placed her hand on Richie's arm. "Maybe I know a lot more than you give me credit for, Richie. You see, I'm only a superstar to those people out there who don't really know me. They just know what we give them and tell them. To me, I'm still plain, simple Caryn Collins from south Georgia. A little girl with a big dream. To my mom and dad, I still just Caryn... my daddy's little girl. To all those people in that room in there, I'm a paycheck, a way to buy food and clothing and maybe travel a lot. And to you, well, I'm a ticket out of everything that ever went wrong in your life. Don't you see, I can't be all those things to all those people. All I am is Caryn Collins—a country girl with traditional values who sings her butt off to try to make a living. I'm no different, no better, than anyone else. If anything, maybe I just try a little harder. That's all I am."

Halloway had melted in Caryn's hands. "Would you really do all of that for me if I promise to let everybody go?"

"I swear it, Richie. You have my word."

"All right, you have a deal. Cliff, Amy, and Ray are painting one of the eighteen-wheelers. As soon as they're done, you can make the calls. When you tell me the money will be transferred and you call the radio station, we'll leave."

Caryn rubbed Richie's arm and smiled with the same soft, affectionate smile that had captured hearts across America. "Good. I think you're making the right choice."

Richie looked into Caryn's captivating eyes. "Will you do one thing, just for me?"

"What's that?"

"Will you sing my song for me . . . just you and me?"

"Sure. I can count on you sticking with your word, can't I?"

"I promise, but you know we'll have to cut the telephone line and disable the other vehicles, don't you?"

"Just don't hurt anyone else, please. I'd rather sing love songs than a death song." Caryn Collins held on to Richie's arm, and she sang to him.

———

Lilly Arthur sat at the second-floor window, looking out into the late afternoon sky. She saw the clouds, laced with red, lazily dancing across the western horizon. She lifted her eyes deep into the heavens above, slid from her chair, and dropped to her knees, her hands clasped beneath her chin. She prayed.

Lilly stayed in that position for several minutes, her eyes opened wide, staring through the window into the peaceful sky. She prayed and then prayed some more. And while she spoke to her God high above in the heavens, she recalled her life before Ray Hartley came into it. The tranquillity and inner peace she and her family had enjoyed was more than anyone, any family, could ask for. Life on the remote Nebraska farm was at times very difficult. But the fruits of the toil made it all worthwhile. Once the farm had glistened with bountiful crops and prime cattle. Once the feeling of heaven on earth had filled the four corners of the modest farmhouse. Once . . . before Ray Hartley came.

She prayed again. "Dear God in Heaven . . . hear me. Deliver me from these evil ones who have come into my life. Stave off the beasts that try to devour me and show me a way out into the comfort of your heavenly arms. Please deliver me to my family and my friends who have come to you before me. My earthly work is finished, and I'm ready to come home, dear God. Show me the way."

And then her eyes saw it. At first she wasn't sure. In the sky. The clouds. She strained her eyes, feeling at first that they were playing tricks on her. And then she knew they weren't. It was there before her, filling the sky. It was as plain as day and just like she had always imagined it would be—like the Bible said it would be. It was awesome, bold, and filled with sadness. It was her Savior's face, and his eyes were looking straight at her.

Lilly Arthur trembled, and the tremble became violent shaking. She bowed her head. "Oh, dear God." Then she jerked her head back up; the clouds were still there. His face was still there, and there was more sadness. She even thought she saw a tear rolling down his cheeks. And like a mighty bolt of lightning, the lips on the face moved and spoke to her. Only her. She listened.

She closed her eyes and prayed aloud. When she opened them again, his image was gone, but his presence was still there. Lilly had heard the message, and she knew that her Savior had delivered her. He had told her what she had to do, and he had shown her the way.

Lilly closed her eyes again and prayed, a long, thankful prayer. When she opened her eyes once more, the clouds had gone, and in their place was the first hint of darkness. She stood and sat back in the chair. She looked at the darkening sky. "Harold . . . Mary Beth, I'm coming home to be with you. Make a place for me. I'm leaving this earthly body behind, and I'm coming to your side at the right hand of our Lord."

Lilly Arthur rose from the chair. She walked unsteadily around the room. Her mind raced back in time—to Mary Beth, Harold. This room had been almost sacred since their deaths. No one had entered it, and nothing had been disturbed since Mary Beth left the world. And she remembered her own simple, humble wedding dress that had been stored for years in the spare closet in one corner of the bedroom. She went to the closet and found the dress. Time had taken its toll on the garment. What had once been pearly white gingham was now faded, tattered, and yellow. She lifted the dress from the crumbling garment bag and spread it carefully on the bed. Then she walked to a mirror on the dresser beside the bed.

When she looked into it, she saw the woman she had known in her youth—plain, yet beautiful. She picked up a hair brush she had given Mary Beth for Christmas years ago. With delicate strokes, she ran the brush through her hair. And like magic, the white hair she had seen for so many years disappeared. In its place there were golden brown locks that flowed and fell into place with every stroke.

Lilly went back to the bed and removed the worn dress she wore. She gently picked up her wedding dress and slipped it on. To her amazement, it fit almost as well as it had so many years ago. She zipped it and stepped back in front of the mirror. Before her eyes was the beautiful bride Harold Arthur had taken for his own, and it made her smile.

She went back to the bed, picked up the worn dress she had removed, and placed it in the garment bag, then crossed unsteadily back to the big closet to hang the garment bag on the clothes rack. When she turned around, she picked up her salvation just as her Savior had told her to do.

Lilly walked back to the bed and turned the covers down. She propped up the pillows, climbed in, and pulled the covers over her just below her breasts. She lay in the bed, half sitting and half lying, against the pillows. Her Savior had shown her the way of her delivery from her earthly shroud. She waited for the evil beast to come and devour her.

CHAPTER FIFTEEN

Richie Halloway stood beside the sofa in the living room. Ray Hartley, Cliff Scott, and Amy Markham sat in chairs around the room. He spoke softly. "Okay, I want to tell all of you this. First, I didn't bring Lionel into this because he's hurt bad. It's all he can do to stay alert in there with those people. Next, I've reached an agreement with Caryn Collins. In a little while, she's going to make a telephone call to her accountant. She'll instruct him to bank-wire three million dollars to an account in Mexico City that will be opened under a fictitious name. I will give her the name. When that is—"

Ray Hartley jumped to his feet. "Are you crazy? You make a telephone call from here, and the cops are gonna swarm in here on top of us. Have you lost your mind?"

"Ray, sit down and shut up. Hear me out. I planned this escape, and I planned the rest of it. I brought all you guys along for different reasons. I promised you a fair share of the take, and I'll stick to that. If you want it, you've got to listen to me and do exactly what I tell you. If anybody—and I mean anybody—screws up, we could all die. Now pay attention."

Cliff Scott looked at Hartley. "Ray, be cool. Let's hear what the man has to say. He's called the shots okay so far. Hear him out. Go on, Rich."

Hartley sat down and cradled his shotgun.

"She's going to have the money wired to Mexico City. You have the rigs painted, right?"

Cliff Scott nodded his head. "Should be dry in an hour or two."

Halloway continued. "Good. At midnight, we're leaving this place. All of us leave except Lionel. He needs medical help. He'll only slow us down."

Hartley was shaking his head. "You mean you're gonna leave Lionel for the cops? Rich, this ain't like you."

"Okay, you don't like my decision about that, let's vote on it. Who wants to take Lionel with us? Raise your hand."

Hartley's hand hit the air, but no one else moved.

"Okay, the decision stands. He stays."

Hartley still wasn't satisfied. "Damn! I don't believe this. You'd leave one of our own?"

Cliff addressed the problem. "Would you rather have him get all of us caught, Ray?"

Hartley thought about it for a moment. "Okay, I guess not. It just don't seem right, that's all. He's earned his share like everybody else. He did his part. He's stayed in that room like a real trooper. It just don't feel right to me, but I'll go along with it."

Richie continued. "All right. Now, when we leave, we'll split up. Two of us in each eighteen-wheeler. We still have enough cash from what I got from Aldridge to get us to Mexico City. We'll meet there in a week from the time we leave. Everybody agree with that?"

Hartley didn't like it. "What happens if somebody doesn't get there? What then?"

Amy Markham spoke up. "Then it's their tough luck."

"Okay, listen to me. Please. We've got to get out of here by midnight. We're out in the country. I figure that even if somebody does manage to trace the call when Collins makes it, it'll take 'em awhile. I mean, did you see that telephone by the kitchen door? It's an antique. These phones probably haven't been upgraded in thirty years."

Hartley jumped back to his feet. "Yeah, Rich. Probably. But what if they have been? What then? I say we leave as soon as we know the call is complete and the bitch has ordered the transfer."

Cliff Scott agreed. "He may have something there, Rich. And what if the broad says its done and it ain't? We got no insurance. I agree with Ray. I say we leave as soon as the call is made and we take Collins with us. We check tomorrow from a pay phone, and if the money is there, we can let her go."

Halloway walked around the small room in a tight circle. He rubbed the back of his head and flexed his neck muscles. "Okay, we'll take her with us. She rides with me and Amy, though. Agreed?"

Everyone nodded.

"Okay, I also promised that if Collins made the call, no one else would be hurt. I intend for everyone to stick with that. No bullshit. Unless somebody is trying to escape or hurt you, no one is to be harmed. We hurt somebody or kill somebody, and the deal is off. Everybody got that? Ray?"

Once more, everyone agreed.

Halloway took a deep breath and continued around the room. "Okay, I got a lot to do. I think it would be a good idea if everyone got some sleep between now and the time we leave. I'm gonna give it until ten o'clock, and then I have Collins make the call. That's two hours from now. I figure the later we leave, the less likely we are to be spotted because there won't be so much traffic on the roads. We can be on Interstate Eighty within an hour from the time we leave. Now go get some shut-eye, and let's get this thing finished. Remember, nobody else gets hurt. We're too damned close to making this work. Nobody screw it up."

———

Wilbur Matthews was taking care of Dennis Goodman while they waited for the Medevac helicopter. Wilbur had found a large flashlight to signal the chopper pilot.

Once Roy O'Connall had unloaded Goodman from the Jeep, he had left the two men at the Matthews farm and returned to where he had last seen Marc Lee. He worked his way through the tall grass until he finally found Marc and Carl lying in the grass and watching the farmyard.

Marc had heard him coming and waited to be sure it

was O'Connall. Once the three men were together, Marc was the first to break the silence. "How's Goodman?"

O'Connall responded in a whisper. "Still unconscious, but I think he might make it. Wilbur's with him, waiting on the chopper. He's got a light to signal the pilot. What's happening here?"

Carl answered. "The dirtbags left the barn a little while ago and went into the house. Haven't seen a thing move since then.'"

O'Connall understood. "What's the plan?"

Marc looked at Carl, then at O'Connall. "A surgical extraction. We go in, get the hostages, and get the hell out. Preferably, there will be no contact with the dirtbags until after the hostages are freed. The one exception might be the person standing guard in the room where the hostages are held. If we're unfortunate enough to encounter the escapees, we terminate them immediately. The hostages are paramount. Don't subject them to unnecessary danger. They've been through enough. I don't give a shit about the dirtbags. Once the hostages are out, we'll handle them as the situation dictates. We'll give them an opportunity to call it quits. If they surrender, they're yours, and we're out of here. If they don't—they'd best commit their souls to their maker because their asses belong to us."

O'Connall almost laughed, but he thought better of it and grinned instead. "I like the way you guys think. What do you want me to do?"

Marc outlined the details of the plan. When he was finished, he illuminated the digital display of his wristwatch. "It's eight-forty-five. If we all get into place quickly and quietly, we can move at exactly eight-fifty. Either of you have any questions before we move out?"

Roy and Carl didn't answer.

"Okay, let's get it done. Safety above all else. Agreed?"

Roy and Carl nodded.

Marc was up, moving toward the barn. He moved the wooden door to open it, then rolled inside. A precaution. He came up on his feet and swept the interior of the barn with the muzzle of the Uzi. Nothing. When he was satisfied that it was clean, he rolled under the eighteen-wheeler that had been repainted by the thugs. He reached to his utility belt and came up with his MiniMaglite. He switched it on and looked into the engine compartment beneath the rig. When he had spotted what he wanted, he took a universal wrench from his utility pants pocket and removed the hex nut that held the battery cable ring-terminal to the starter. That finished, he went to the next one. When the second vehicle was disabled, Marc slid from beneath it and moved to the front door of the barn.

Carl Browne had worked his way through the tall grass to the west of the farmhouse. He made an oval loop and got himself into position a hundred feet from the house at the rear. He looked at his watch. Two minutes to go.

Roy O'Connall had never participated in an operation quite like this one before. Right now, it was fun, but he had an idea that the fun would abruptly stop at the sound of the first gunshot if the attack was detected. He moved through the grass east of the barn and farmhouse, working his way to the blind side of the springhouse. He stopped to evaluate the situation.

Marc's synopsis had been correct. There was a totally blind corner behind the springhouse. O'Connall broke into a hard run for the cover of the springhouse. When he reached it, he worked around to the western corner and dropped into position. He could see the front porch, the entire front wall, and the northern wall of the house. His right index finger eased the safety block forward on the Mini-14. He took a deep breath and checked his wrist-watch. One minute until penetration.

Marc slipped through the front door of the weathered barn and moved into the open. This was the critical moment, the best chance to die. He ran to the tall grass to the west, toward Carl. Once he was at the rear corner of the farmhouse, he broke into a zigzag run for the northern wall. When he reached it, he leaned in close to the wall and checked his watch. Thirty seconds.

Carl was moving fast. He came alongside Marc, his Uzi cradled against his chest. They stood side-by-side against the wall. Fifteen seconds.

Marc moved to the window of the room that held the

hostages. He had dropped to a low crouch to keep out of sight. Ten seconds.

Carl moved in directly behind Marc. Both highway warriors hugged the wall of the old farmhouse. Five seconds. Four. Three.

Showtime.

Marc stood up fast. He looked through the broken window at the hostages scattered throughout the room. In a microsecond, his eyes landed on Lionel Lewis, who held his submachine gun haphazardly against his side. Lewis's left side was toward Marc, his other side toward the door. There was no way Lewis could see the merchant of death ready to tap on his shoulder.

Marc put his left index finger against his lips for silence. At least five or six of the hostages had seen him, but no one uttered a sound.

He immediately leveled the Uzi at Lewis and squeezed the trigger for a controlled three-round burst of silent, flaming death. The 9-mm jacketed death rounds slammed into Lewis's side with enough ferocity to shove him toward the far wall. His subgun clattered to the floor, followed by Lewis's trembling dead body.

Marc was over the edge of the window now. He climbed inside, and every face in the room turned pale. His left index finger was once again over his lips. Then he pointed at the window and motioned for everyone to move. He watched as the first of the hostages scurried through the broken glass and jumped to safety. Marc kept his Uzi pointed at the doorway that led back into the house. He turned and motioned for the hostages to hurry.

Outside, Carl helped the captives cross the threshhold into freedom. He eased them to the ground and pointed the way for them to follow. He had whispered to the first one to get to the edge of the grass and help the others get to the tall grassy knoll behind the barn. The captive led the way to safety while Carl covered him.

Roy O'Connall watched the procession of captives leave the house. A smile of satisfaction crossed his face. But before he could get too caught up in the excitement, he let his eyes drift back to the front door and the porch.

He was pleased because so far, the rescue was coming off with clockwork precision.

Marc glanced around one more time. There were five captives left. He moved toward the window behind them, the Uzi still sweeping the only door into the room. When the last hostage moved through the shattered window, Marc climbed out behind him.

Carl was already moving with the last few hostages. They moved through the tall grass in a steady line. And still, no one had spoken a word.

Marc stopped at the edge of the grass with the last hostage. "Which one is Caryn Collins?"

For a second, the hostage seemed puzzled, as if he expected Marc to know the answer to the question. "Uh, she wasn't in there. They took her out into the main part of the house a few minutes before you came."

———

Ray Hartley jumped from the sofa where he had been sleeping, his voice excited. "What was that?"

Cliff Scott rolled over on the floor and rubbed his eyes. "What's wrong with you, Ray?"

Hartley stumbled around the living room. "A noise. I heard a noise outside. Like a motor, an engine. Maybe one of the buses."

Scott sat up. "You're dreamin', man. I don't hear anything."

Hartley was adamant. "I'm tellin' you, I heard a motor start up. Where is everybody?"

"We're all right here except Lionel. He's still in the back room."

Hartley grabbed the Remington 870 and moved to the front window. "Where's Rich?"

Richie Halloway bolted through the doorway between the kitchen and the living room. "What's goin' on in here?"

Hartley turned. "I heard something like a motor running. Something's goin' on outside."

Richie strained to listen. "I don't hear nothin'. Maybe you had a dream."

Hartley came back to the sofa. "Bullshit! I'm tellin' you, I heard something outside. Somebody's out there."

Halloway nonchalantly shrugged. "Okay, Ray, whatever you say. We're all a little edgy, but it's almost over. Twenty-four hours from now, we'll have more money than we can spend. It's nerves, man. If it'll make you feel better, take a walk to the barn and look around."

Hartley cradled the Remington and went to the door. "I think I'll do that. I'm going out to the barn."

He opened the door and stepped onto the porch into a peaceful and tranquil country night. Two steps onto the porch, the tranquillity was shattered by lights more brilliant than sunlight. Hartley froze.

A voice unlike any he had ever heard boomed across the damp country air on a loudspeaker. "Stop where you are! Release Lilly Arthur and Caryn Collins. Throw down your weapons and come out. We will not harm you."

Hartley answered the demands with a shotgun burst into the light nearest him. He spun around and dived back through the open front door into the living room, his heart racing. He slammed the front door closed and stopped near the sofa, on his knees taking cover.

Outside, behind the safety of the springhouse, Marc Lee laid the microphone back down on the mixing console beside the idling bus. He spoke over the hum of the auxiliary generator. "I don't think he liked my suggestion. It's time he experienced some of the alternatives."

Richie Halloway was in a panic. "What's goin' on? What are those lights?"

Cliff Scott jumped to his feet, grabbed his shotgun, and moved beside Amy who was already coming up from her place on the floor. When he looked at Richie, his face was molded in fear. "We've had it. They've found us."

Amy was yelling. "Cut the lights. Hurry! Get the lights off so they can't see inside."

Halloway shouted orders. "Ray, cover the front. Cliff, go check on Lionel and the hostages. Be sure everything's all right back there."

Scott nodded and disappeared down the hallway.

Halloway wasn't finished. "Amy, look around and find some quilts or blankets—anything to cover the windows."

"Right." Amy hit the steps to the second floor on a run.

Cliff screamed from the back of the house. "Rich! Hurry! Get back here."

Halloway ran down the hallway. When he stepped through the doorway, his heart sank, and he felt like he was going to throw up. The same feeling rushed over him that he had felt when the judge read his sentence. Cliff Scott was dazed. The room was empty, except for Lionel's body and the body of Mike Coble. "Oh, shit!" said Halloway. "What's happened here? Who did this to me?"

"I did!" Marc Lee answered from outside the open window.

Scott spun around and fired a wasted shotgun blast toward the shattered window. He and Halloway made a frantic dive for the open door and landed in the hallway outside the room.

Halloway yelled into the room. "Who are you?"

There was no answer.

Halloway and Scott ran back to the living room, their faces pale. "They're gone. All of 'em. Gone."

Caryn Collins screamed. "They're dead? My friends are dead?"

"No, dammit. Gone. Vanished. All of 'em. And Lionel is dead. Who are these people?"

Amy returned from the second floor, hysterical. "We've got to get out of here."

Caryn Collins looked at Richie Halloway in the dim glow of the hall light. "Give it up, Richie? Please, before someone else dies."

Ray Hartley screamed angrily, "Give up—never. Not as long as there's breath in my body. I came here to take care of unfinished business, and that's exactly what I'm going to do. After that, I don't give a shit." He hit the steps toward Lilly Arthur.

Halloway's voice trembled, and his body shook. "We're all in too deep. We gotta see this through."

Caryn pleaded. "It doesn't have to be like this, Richie. Quit now."

Cliff Scott was frantic. "Shut up, bitch. We escaped

from a maximum-security prison, we can sure as hell get out of this."

Halloway was scared out of his mind and confused. "All of you just shut up for a minute. Leave me alone and let me think."

Amy couldn't take any more. "While you're thinkin', I'm haulin' ass. You goin', Cliff?"

Cliff hesitated. "What? How? You can't just walk out there. They'll kill you."

Amy was determined. "That's better than dyin' in this rathole."

"Please, Amy—don't do it."

"I gotta, Cliff. Just like I had to help you escape. I gotta do it." She ran to the back of the house, pried a southside window open with her gun stock, and slipped through it. She hit the ground running, her eyes focused on the edge of the field and the tall grass. Ten feet into the grass, she tripped, crashed violently to the ground, and lost her grip on the handgun. She struggled to find the gun, to get up, but Roy O'Connall's voice stopped her cold. "Are you sure you're not Diane Morgan?"

Amy trembled, looking up into the darkness while her hand swept the ground for the gun. "You bastard!"

"Nope, name's O'Connall. Roy O'Connall. The game's over. You lose!"

Amy found the gun and swung it around, but a massive left hook sent her reeling into mental darkness.

O'Connall cuffed Amy's hands behind her back. "Dirtbags never learn."

Inside the house, Ray Hartley unlocked the door to Lilly Arthur's room. He opened it, switched the overhead light on, and stepped inside.

Lilly Arthur was in the bed wearing a tattered dress, her hair sticking out wildly in all directions. Her eyes were open wide, too wide, as if she were possessed by some spirit, and she was smiling. Hartley stopped cold. "You crazy old bitch. You've lost your mind."

Lilly didn't answer, and she didn't move.

"That's okay. It's all over now. Time to finish what I started nine years ago. You're dead, old woman. I'm gonna cut you to pieces, and then I'm gonna shoot what's left of you until I'm sure this time you're dead." He moved to the end of the bed and stopped again.

Lilly Arthur still didn't move. "You're evil, Ray Hartley. You're nothin' more than the devil incarnate. Hell's waitin' for you."

Hartley laughed. "Preach to me, old woman. Preach loud and mean. I want to hear you preachin' when I cut your throat." Hartley produced a large knife. The Remington shotgun was aimed at Lilly's chest.

"Ray Hartley, the wages of your sins is death. You die for what you've done!"

"Yeah, yeah, that's it. Preach to me. Preach to me!" He moved his arm up to strike with the knife. His finger moved back on the shotgun's trigger.

Lilly Arthur didn't change her smile. "Death, Ray Hartley. The devil's callin' for your soul."

The bed covers jumped and a thunderous roar shook the room as flying buckshot caught Hartley in the chest. The shotgun flew from his hands, firing a wasted load of buckshot into the foot of the bed. His body jerked violently backward from the impact. His eyes opened wide, but he didn't go down. He moved forward again, screaming, "You killed me! You killed me!"

Another roar of thunder vibrated the walls and silenced Ray Hartley. His body slammed against the blood-splattered wall behind him and collapsed forever.

Lilly Arthur pulled the smoking, rusted old double-barrel shotgun from beneath the now ragged covers. She laid it gently on the floor and leaned back against the pillows. Her face was split wide with satisfaction, and she closed her eyes.

Momentarily, the smile faded, her head listed to one side, and Lilly Arthur went home to her family.

Downstairs, Cliff Scott knew he had to do something fast. He grabbed Caryn Collins around the neck with his left arm and crammed the sawed-off shotgun into her kidneys with his right. He started for the door. "We're goin' out of here. You comin', Rich?"

Halloway didn't know what to do. "Oh, man, not this way."

"I'm leavin', Rich. Now!" Scott opened the front door.

Marc Lee had moved into position on the south side of the front porch. He had ordered the lights extinguished and instructed the roadie to switch them back on when he saw movement from the house. Marc's Uzi was ready to breathe fire and death.

Carl had found cover behind a thick rosebush forty or fifty feet out in the front yard. He waited.

Cliff Scott took three steps into the yard, and the night lit up with blinding intensity. He froze in his tracks. "We're goin' out of here. I mean it. I'll blow her in half." He started walking again, Richie Halloway closely beside him.

Marc leveled the Uzi's sights on Scott. "Give it up. There's nowhere for you to go. We have you surrounded."

Scott nudged the shotgun further into Caryn's ribs. He yelled, "Get the hell back. We're goin' to the buses. You get in our way, and she dies."

Marc steadied his aim, but the Uzi's sights weren't designed for sniper work. A shot would be far too risky. "Let her go. There's no way you can escape."

Scott's voice echoed through the Nebraska night. "Go ahead, hero. Try it. You may take one of us. You might even get lucky and take both of us. Then again, our fingers just might twitch, and it's bye-bye bitch. Clear the way to the barn." Scott stopped and scanned the yard. "Do it now!"

Carl took careful aim. He knew he could take one of the gunmen, but he also knew Scott was right. A dying twitch or muscle spasm, and Caryn Collins was hamburger. He yelled at Scott instead. "Listen to the man, dude. You ain't goin' nowhere 'cept maybe to hell. Don't make it any worse on yourselves. Let the lady go and put down your weapons. We don't want to hurt you."

Marc tried a distraction. "Where's Hartley? You leave him inside to face the music alone?"

"He's dead. The old woman killed him," Halloway yelled. "We don't want to hurt Caryn. I mean that. Just get out of our way and let us out of here."

Marc's voice was firm. "I'm sorry, Richie. I can't do that."

Roy O'Connall lay prone at the edge of the grass. He

lifted the modified Ruger Mini-14 to eye level and squinted through the peep sight. He found Scott's head and gently nudged the safety forward. He eased back on the trigger, but then he stopped. From his angle, he could put a bullet right into Scott's ear. Problem was, the 55-grain full-metal-jacket rounds he was using were notorious for tumbling once they'd ripped through flesh. In all likelihood, the bullet would strike Scott, terminate him, and tumble through his head until it took out Caryn Collins standing on the other side. O'Connall slipped the safety back on and let the weapon rest. Then he mumbled under his breath, "Come on, you bastard, move just six inches. Please, just six inches, and I'll take the top of your head off."

Scott and Halloway didn't move. They were frozen, partly from fear and partly from indecision. One thing both of the outlaws knew well. They weren't going back to the joint. No way.

Halloway yelled out, "You've got one minute to bring a bus here. I want Bernie Aldridge to drive. That bus ain't beside us when I call time, and we'll kill her. I swear it, we'll kill her."

"You do that, Richie, and we'll kill you before she hits the ground. That's *my* promise," Marc yelled.

Halloway's voice quivered. "I don't know who you are, mister. There's something you'd better know. Me and Cliff—well—it don't matter to us anymore. Me and him died years ago when they shut that steel door behind us."

Scott agreed. "He's right, mister. We got nothin' left to lose. The lady here does, and her clock's runnin' out. What's it gonna be?"

CHAPTER SIXTEEN

Roy O'Connall had already started moving when he realized there was no way he could get a shot without jeopardizing Caryn Collins's life. He circled the house on Scott and Halloway's blind side and moved near the rosebush where Carl had taken cover. "I'm headin' for the Vette, just in case they get out of here."

Carl kept his eyes on the deadly escapees. "Good move. We gotta let 'em out, or Collins is over. If we can get 'em on the road, I think we have a better chance of freeing Collins. Haul ass. Wait, take this." Carl handed O'Connall the Icom hand-held radio. "Stay in touch with Marc on that. I'll have contact when I get to the Jeep. Whatever you do, don't lose 'em if they roll before I get to the Cherokee."

"Not a chance," O'Connall said, taking the radio.

The Icom speaker crackled with Marc's voice. "Bro, you listenin'?"

O'Connall handed the radio back to Carl.

"Go," Carl said.

"Let's give 'em the bus. Move to the Cherokee as fast as you can and get back to the main road," Marc said.

Carl talked as he scrambled toward the barn, O'Connall directly behind him. "Roger. I'm giving O'Connall the hand-held. He's headed for his Vette. What about you?"

"The bus has a ladder to the roof down the back. I'll hitch a ride when they leave. Don't worry about me, I'll be hanging around. Get back to the rig and be prepared to move when we pass you. Let O'Connall follow 'em out, and then he can take the lead when we get to the main road—if it goes that far."

"Roger," Carl said, and he handed the radio back to O'Connall. "Let's do it, and good luck."

O'Connall grinned. "Yeah, you too." He disappeared into the darkness.

Scott yelled a final warning. "So what's it gonna be?"

Marc answered. "You got your bus. Be patient. It'll take a few minutes to warm up."

"Screw that. Get that damned bus down here now!" Scott yelled.

"It's coming," Marc yelled. He hoped the roadies took the cue and prepared the bus.

They did.

The sound of the big diesel bus engine roared through the night. It took two minutes, but the bus finally entered the sea of light in the front yard, Bernie at the wheel. It stopped beside Scott, Halloway, and Caryn Collins. The door opened.

Marc Lee started his mental timer. When the bus moved forward, the lights would be switched off. He would have to move carefully and swiftly. A miscalculation, and both he and Caryn could very well be dead.

Richie Halloway spun around with his shotgun and swept the steps leading into the bus. He moved up them cautiously, the muzzle of the shotgun trained on Bernie Aldridge's head. "Anybody else on this bus besides you, Bernie?"

"No," Aldridge said, trembling.

"You better not be lyin'. I find anybody else on here, and I'm gonna waste all of you." Halloway moved through the bus, the barrel of the sawed-off shotgun sweeping the area in front of him and to each side as he walked. He checked each berth, bunk, and nook until he reached the master suite in the rear of the bus. Halloway shoved the door with his foot and dropped low when it swung open. He swept the suite with the shotgun muzzle.

Nothing.

Halloway moved back to Bernie Aldridge. He stuck the shotgun into Bernie's neck. "We're leavin' this place. You or anybody else try something heroic, and you're history. Remember, Bernie: I don't like you very much. Give me half a reason, and I'll blow your head off. Got that?"

Aldridge nodded.

"Good," Halloway said. He looked around the yard. All he could see was lights. No people. He looked at Cliff, who had moved against the side of the bus with Caryn Collins still in front of him. "Okay, Cliff. It's clear."

Scott tightened his grip around Caryn's neck. He moved to the steps and backed up them. When he got inside, he shouted orders at Bernie. "Close the door and get this thing out of here. Try anything cute, you and this broad are history. Get movin'!"

Aldridge did as he was told. He pressed the clutch to the floor and moved the gearshift into low. He pressed the accelerator and let the clutch out slowly. The bus crept forward.

Scott shoved Caryn into a lounge seat in front of the bus. He sat across the aisle in another seat and rested the shotgun across his legs, the muzzle pointed directly at Caryn, his index finger squarely on the trigger.

The bus rocked as it crossed the uneven farmyard, tossing its occupants from side to side.

Scott glanced out the window. "Keep an eye out, Rich. Make sure nobody is followin' us."

Halloway looked out the window. "Cliff, maybe you'd better go to the back and be sure nobody is back there."

Caryn Collins spoke up. "Save yourself a trip. There are no windows in the back of the bus. You can't see anything."

"Shit!" Halloway said. "Maybe we should have taken the van, Cliff."

"No way, man. The van might be faster on these little roads, but get this big bus up to speed on the highway, and there is no way they can stop us."

Halloway wasn't convinced. "What if they set up roadblocks or something?"

Scott laughed. "Not a chance. They'd have to make us crash to stop us, and they wouldn't want to risk getting Miss Prettyface hurt. She's our ticket to freedom."

Caryn felt helpless. "What are you going to do with us?"

Halloway answered. "That depends on those people

out there. They leave us alone until we get to Mexico City, then you can take your bus and go home. They don't, well . . ."

Caryn's face turned ashen. "You mean you'd really kill us?"

Halloway's face turned to stone. "In a heartbeat."

The bus inched forward and then shook from side to side as it rolled onto the gravel lane. A loud thud came from the back.

Halloway jerked around. "What was that?"

"Be cool, Rich. We hit the gravel, that's all. Man, you're so nervous, you might shoot old Bernie before he gets us to the road."

Aldridge cowered down but kept his hands on the steering wheel. "Which way you want me to go when we get to the road?"

"Left," Scott said. "Follow the road until we tell you to turn. I don't care what's in front of you—don't you stop this bus for anything. You got that?"

Aldridge nodded.

"Good. Drive," Scott said.

The bright lights outside went off. Scott jerked to attention, and Halloway looked hard out of the window.

"Hey, Cliff, what happened?"

"They turned the lights off. Nothing to worry about. Ain't nothing there to look at now."

Marc Lee made a hard run from his cover at the corner of the house. He reached the rear of the bus and sprinted to catch it. He was well onto the gravel lane when his hand caught the chrome ladder rail up the back of the bus. He lunged for the bottom rung and climbed quickly to the top. Once there, he moved onto the roof and held tightly to one of the cargo rails that lined either side. The bus bounced and groaned on the gravel road, but Marc held tightly. He looked for a way to get inside the vehicle, but he couldn't see anything. He looked for a way to get to the front near the windshield, but the cargo railing stopped halfway from the rear.

The bus slowed and then turned onto the main gravel road at the end of the lane. Marc, spread-eagled on the roof, held on for the ride.

———

Roy O'Connall was out of breath when he reached his ZR-1 Corvette. On the run, he hadn't heard the sound of the bus engine, and he hoped that meant the bus hadn't gotten past him. He unlocked the door and tossed his Ruger Mini-14 into the passenger's seat. He climbed in, laid the Icom hand-held on the dash, and fired the engine. The Corvette rumbled to life.

O'Connall slipped the gearshift into *reverse* and tapped the accelerator. The mighty LT-4 engine roared, and the Vette leapt backward in a wake of dirt and dust. Roy pulled the headlight switch. The headlamp bays popped open and locked. The Vette's high-intensity quartz-halogen lights cast a hot-white light on the field in front of him.

O'Connall steered hard right, and the Vette swung left. He slapped the brakes and dropped the gearshift into *drive*. His foot tapped the accelerator, and the powerful power plant lunged the Vette forward. Roy twisted and turned until he saw the main gravel road ahead. He dropped the gearshift into *neutral,* cut the lights, lowered the windows, and waited.

He heard it—a roar at first—and then he saw head-lights. He watched the lights, but something didn't look right. They were too low, and the silhouette was too small. Just as he determined that, Carl streaked past him in the Jeep Cherokee.

O'Connall picked up the radio from the dash and pressed the transmit switch. "This is O'Connall. Either of you guys know where they are?"

"Roger," Carl said. "They're behind me. I saw head-lights when I came onto the road. I took a shortcut through the field. Marc should have contact. You there, Colonel? Over."

Marc's voice was difficult to understand because of the wind noise in the microphone. "Affirmative. I'm on the roof, and we're moving east on the main gravel road. Should be about two hundred yards from the farm's driveway now. It's a rough ride up here on top. Over."

Carl came on the air. "You copy that, O'Connall?"

"Yeah, ten-four. I got it. What's the plan?"

Marc answered. "Fall in behind the bus when it passes you. Carl, get to the rig and get loaded. We're ten to fifteen minutes away if Aldridge doesn't get a lead foot. Carl, fall in the rear when we pass the rig. They shouldn't suspect it. O'Connall, you take the lead. Don't make it too obvious you're tagging them until I give the word. We screw up, and two more innocent people are gonna die. I'll search for a way inside from here. We'll have to make our timing precise, or we'll blow it. I'll keep in touch from here. Everybody got that? Over?"

"O'Connall, roger."

"Got it, Colonel," Carl said. "You give the word and we'll take 'em down. A rolling takedown should work fine on this one. Over."

"Affirmative. We have no margin for error. When we take the bus down, we have to liberate the hostages within seconds if we want to avoid innocent casualties. I'll know when the time is right, so hang with me. I'm out."

Marc's voice had hardly stopped coming from the speaker when O'Connall saw the bus moving along the road. He sat patiently until it passed him. He let them take a good lead, and then he dropped the Vette into gear. Dust flew in his wake when he hit the gravel road. The Vette fishtailed, but a sharp twist on the steering wheel straightened it. Loose gravel slapped the undercarriage, creating rifle-shot pops. O'Connall ignored it and moved in as close as he dared—three hundred yards. He left his headlights off and followed the bus by using its taillights for guidance. He keyed the hand-held transmitter. "I'm on them now, Carl. We're rolling in your direction. Can you see me, Marc? Over."

"Negative," Marc said. "Didn't even know you were there yet. Over."

"Good," O'Connall replied. "Over."

Carl's voice projected from the speaker. "Hang tight, both of you. I'm five minutes from the rig. I'm giving it all I can on this loose gravel. I'll be ready when you pass. Over."

"Roger," Roy said. He laid the hand-held back on the dashboard and concentrated on driving.

Inside the customized show bus, Bernie Aldridge was so scared he could hardly breathe. It took every ounce of courage and strength to drive the bus. His attention focused on the shotgun barrel pressed against his neck rather than the road in front of him.

The road made a sharp bend to the right, and Aldridge wasn't ready for it. The bus was halfway into the turn before he realized it. He panicked and cut hard on the steering wheel. The bus rocked and groaned, skidded. Aldridge let off the accelerator and hit the brakes—wrong move. The bus skidded hard now, out of control. It was sideways through the turn, listing hard to the left. Aldridge fought for control to keep the mammoth vehicle from overturning.

Caryn Collins screamed.

Richie Halloway was thrown from his seat, the shotgun flying wildly from his hands as he struggled for balance.

Cliff Scott's head slammed into the window beside him, but he held firmly to his shotgun.

On top of the bus, Marc Lee struggled for survival. The wild careening turn caused him to lose his grip on the right cargo rail. He slid hard to the left side and crashed into the tiny metal rail that served as his only barrier against certain death.

Marc's weight, driven by the centrifugal force that slammed him to the outer edge, was more than the railing could handle. It snapped, broken pieces plunging to the gravel below.

Marc sailed over the edge of the roof like a flat rock skipping on water. In a desperate effort to survive this night, he grabbed at the remaining section of railing. His right hand found metal, and his body slammed violently into the side of the bus. He fought to hold on, his arm aching from the torturous sudden strain. If the bus rolled over, he would be pinned beneath it, crushed like a bug.

Marc's feet scrambled for a foothold, but the smooth aluminum skin of the bus offered nothing. His left arm throbbed, and he felt his grip loosening, but he knew he had to hold on. He flopped around on the side of the bus, dangling like a dried leaf fighting autumn winds, clinging by a weakened stem to its only life-support system. He lunged with his right arm as best he could, trying to make it find the security of the railing.

It didn't work. The surge intensified the pain in his left arm. Marc kicked again and scrambled for survival.

Cliff Scott righted himself in the lounge seat and tried to stand, but the bus was still out of control.

Bernie Aldridge cut the steering wheel hard and let off the brake. The bus groaned, righted itself, then rocked to a stop.

Scott was on his feet, screaming and waving the muzzle of the sawed-off shotgun in Aldridge's face. "You stupid shit! I should blow your brains out. Rich, get off your ass and get up here."

Richie Halloway found his shotgun on the steps beside the door. He dusted himself off and moved into the lounge directly behind the driver's seat. His voice was deathly cold. "Look, Cliff. I'm not taking orders from you. If it weren't for me, you'd still be rotting in prison. This is my show. I run it. You don't like it, you get out."

Scott swung the barrel of the shotgun around and leveled it at Halloway. "No, no. You'll do what I say, or I'll waste all three of you. I don't need you anymore. Get your ass in that seat and watch these people. I'll drive the damned bus."

Halloway was frozen. He looked at Scott and then the muzzle of the shotgun. "You sure you want me behind you?"

Scott grinned. "You may be dumb, but you ain't stupid. You need me a hell of a lot more than I need you. Why? Cause I got balls, and you need somebody with balls because you don't have any. Try to take me, and you'd better blow the top of my head off with the first shot. If you don't, the second shot's mine."

Halloway stood expressionless.

"Difference between me and you, Rich, is I ain't scared of dying. It don't matter to me anymore."

———

Marc Lee struggled for stability and found none. His left arm was numb. Since the bus had stopped, he considered dropping to the ground and then climbing back up the ladder at the rear. He dismissed the thought; there was too much possibility of someone looking into the rearview mirror and seeing him. He found one final surge of strength and pulled hard with his left arm while his feet clawed at the slick surface of the bus.

———

Roy O'Connall had slowed the ZR-1 Corvette the instant he saw the taillights on the bus disappear in a cloud of dust. He knew the bus was in trouble, but he decided to hold back and wait for word from Marc. When that word didn't come, he moved in for a closer look.

Had it not been for the backlight from the bus's headlights, O'Connall couldn't have seen anything. As it was, he had a good view of the bus sitting haphazardly in the middle of the gravel road. That's when he saw Marc dangling from the railing on the roof. O'Connall felt helpless. There was no way to help Marc without jeopardizing the lives of Bernie Aldridge and Caryn Collins. O'Connall was relieved when he saw Marc kick his way back on top of the bus. Then, just as suddenly as the mishap had occurred, the bus was moving again.

O'Connall guessed that Aldridge wasn't driving any longer because the bus was traveling much faster than before. He grabbed the Icom radio and made a call. "Carl, you hear me?"

"Yeah, go."

"They're coming your way fast. I think they've changed drivers. Are you ready? Over?"

"I'm set, O'Connall. Let 'em roll," Carl said.

O'Connall keyed the transmitter once more. "Marc, are you okay? I saw you had a little problem. You hang out in the craziest places. Over."

"I'm okay, O'Connall. My arm hurts like hell, but other than that, I'm okay. I'm going to chance a move around on top and see if I can find any way to get inside. I'll be in touch," Marc said. "Over."

The bus was gaining speed now. O'Connall glanced at his digital speedometer—sixty miles per hour. He had closed the gap to the bus, but stayed back two hundred yards.

They hit pavement.

A minute passed, and the tiny sign for Thedford, Nebraska, went by in a blur. O'Connall looked to his left and caught a glimpse of the Leeco over-road rig when they passed.

Carl's voice crackled over the Icom hand-held. "Give me one minute and take the lead, O'Connall. I got 'em from back here. Marc, systems are armed and functional. You give the word and we can take 'em down in a heartbeat. Over."

"Roger," Marc said. "We've got to get those hostages out of there first, if there's any way we can."

Carl ran the rig through the gears, and the giant Caterpillar 1400-horsepower engine hummed. It took less than thirty seconds to catch the speeding bus.

O'Connall switched on his headlights and floored the accelerator. The Vette came to life, and the LT-4 engine roared like thunder. The rear end of the Vette squatted low, and the front end rose high as the state-of-the-art power plant extracted every possible horsepower from the fuel.

O'Connall cut into the passing lane on the narrow two-lane highway. He streaked past Caryn Collins's show bus. He kept that pace until he was well in front of the bus, but it was still visible in his rearview mirror.

Carl moved in close now. He paced it manually and then set the distance on the rig's collision-avoidance system. He let off the accelerator and let the on-board computer do the rest. The CAS and the obstacle-detection system coupled with a device similar to a cruise control on an automobile. The CAS and ODS would do everything but steer the rig.

Carl ran a fast computerized systems analysis of the Leeco rig's technologically advanced weapons systems. A total functional check and recheck took two and a half seconds. The split computer screen flashed: ARMED and READY. Carl pressed the manual override switch and laid the electronic firing trigger over his leg.

The bus turned right and headed south on U.S. 83, directly behind Roy O'Connall in the Vette. Carl turned the rig right, and the electronic systems maintained both distance and speed. The digital electronic speed indicator climbed to eighty and held steady.

Marc struggled against the heavy winds from the sustained high speed. He fumbled frantically with a top-mounted Coleman air conditioner, but the unit was firmly mounted in the roof of the bus. After a few minutes of failed ingenuity, he picked up the Icom hand-held.

"Okay, guys, there's no way to get in from up here, short of blasting a hole. We gotta take 'em down. Carl, move up alongside the bus and hold steady. Roy, drop your speed and slow in front of the bus. Be careful, guys, these people got nothing to lose. Over."

Carl and O'Connall acknowledged.

Carl moved the Leeco rig alongside the show bus. He held steady and gave a long blast on the air horn. He waved at the driver and sounded the air horn again.

Cliff Scott didn't know what to do. "What's with that guy? He's nuts."

Caryn said, "He's probably a fan, and that's his way of saying hello. It happens all the time when we're on the road. Just wave back at him."

Scott waved and pushed harder on the accelerator.

O'Connall dropped back. He slowed until the bus caught up with him. A glance into his rearview mirror told him the bus wasn't slowing. He sped up again, let the bus catch him, and slowed once more.

Cliff Scott didn't slow the bus.

O'Connall sped up and disappeared from sight. He grabbed the hand-held. "Okay, guys. What's next? This ain't gonna work. Crazy bastard would run right over me. Over."

Carl answered. "He won't run over me. I'll cut in front and hold the speed. You drop back and then fall in behind. When you see me brake down, take out the rear tires. I'll stop the bus with the rig. The instant they're stopped, lay some cover fire at the driver, and we'll take 'em down. And O'Connall, shoot high so we don't chance hurting the hostages. Over."

"Got it," O'Connall said. "Over."

"That okay with you, Colonel?" Carl asked. "Over."

"Roger," Marc said. "I've got about seventy-five feet

of rope in my utility pack. I'll tie off on the front air conditioner. The instant we stop, I'll fly in for a little surprise. Let's get it done."

Carl moved the Leeco rig ahead of the bus. He kept the speed steady for several miles so O'Connall could drop behind. But it didn't go right. O'Connall had to pull off the road and wait for the Leeco rig and the bus to pass. He taxed the Corvette's engine until he caught up.

Carl slowed, and Cliff Scott tried to pass. Carl blocked him. Scott rammed the rear of the Leeco rig. When the rig shook, Carl slammed on the brakes. The bus crashed into the titanium-steel bumper on the back of the Leeco trailer.

O'Connall lowered his passenger's window and opened fire into the bus's rear tires.

Scott lost control, and the bus swerved hard right off the highway, onto the shoulder. A hundred yards later, it rocked to a stop, the front of the bus pressed tightly against the rear of the Leeco trailer.

Cliff Scott tried to find *reverse* on the gearshift. He couldn't. He went for his shotgun when the right window behind Caryn Collins disintegrated.

Marc Lee burst through the glass with his silenced Uzi, searching for a target.

Caryn Collins screamed and plunged to the floor.

Richie Halloway was so stunned he hesitated, a fatal mistake. He spun his shotgun toward Marc, but before his finger could work the trigger, a silent streak of blazing 9-mm hellfire tore through his chest and burned his life away. The shotgun flew wildly from his hands, discharging in the process. The wild load of buckshot caught Bernie Aldridge squarely in the rump as he cowered under a seat. He wailed in pain.

Cliff Scott panicked, opened the door, and ran as hard as he could into the darkness.

Marc hit the quick disconnect on the rope and headed out the door after him, but Scott was already lost in the darkness.

Marc shouted into the hand-held, "Scott's out to the right. I've lost him."

"I haven't," Carl said. "Got him on the infrared, forty meters to the right. I'll take him."

Carl pressed buttons and hit switches. The night came alive with the sound of his voice over a public address system. "Cliff Scott. Surrender. There's nowhere for you to run. I've got you tracked electronically. It's over."

Scott replied with two fast ineffective rounds from his shotgun.

"Have it your way, asshole," Carl said. He pressed the firing mechanism for the side-mounted Stinger miniguns, and the rapid-fire machine guns chattered out one second of lightning-fast 5.56-mm death. There was a brief scream from the field beside the road and then silence.

Roy climbed aboard the bus, ready to fire at anything that moved. This time, though, he'd missed all the action.

Toward the rear of the bus, Caryn was bending over Bernie Aldridge.

"Those sons of bitches shot me!" Bernie cried. "Right in the damned keester!"

"Just a flesh wound," Marc assured him. "You'll be okay."

"That's good," Caryn said, "because as soon as he's better, I'm going to sue what's left of his ass off."

"I'm dying, and she's making jokes," Bernie muttered.

"Looks like our work here is done," Marc said. "Roy, you better call in for an ambulance for our friend here. Carl, let's move."

"I'm with you, bro."

As they made their way off the bus, Roy looked first at Marc, then at Carl. "Just tell me one thing. Who the hell *are* you guys?"

"Every criminal's worst nightmare," Marc said.

ACTION ON EIGHTEEN WHEELS!

Marc Lee and Carl Browne, ex-Delta Force commandos and now the men of Overload, are about to tackle their most brutal and bizarre assignment yet—to stem the wholesale slaughter of truckers in Missouri and Arkansas! Law enforcement officials are helpless . . . and now truckers are about to revolt. Nationwide disaster looms ahead, so it's up to Lee and Browne to save the day!

Here's an exciting preview of Book #7 in the explosive OVERLOAD series

MISSOURI MASSACRE
by Bob Ham

Look for OVERLOAD wherever Bantam Books are sold.

Chapter One

1988

Larry Cummings awakened the very instant the alarm clock rang. He reached over to the small stand inside the Freightliner sleeper and shut off the clanging bell. His arms flew out and downward as he stretched them and his legs. Then he rolled over in the bunk and peeked outside. It was raining hard. The third storm in less than six hours.

Cummings thought about getting something to eat at the truckstop restaurant across the lot, but one glance at his watch and he decided against it. He was already ten hours behind schedule. But come hell or high water, he was determined to get the load to the consignee on time. And that meant breaking the speed limits, but that's what the bird dog was for. When the little Escort radar detector chirped, it was foot off the pedal and easy down on the brakes. A few changes in the log book would satisfy even the most discriminating Interstate Commerce commission inspection. No big deal, really, because everybody did it when they got a little off the beaten path of the assigned destination . . . at least everybody *he* hung around with.

When he threw off the blanket, Cummings saw the little brown vial he always kept under the mattress. He had forgotten to tuck it away when he finished with it last night. He picked it up and popped the plastic top. His index finger dipped inside and came out covered with off-white powder. He touched it to his tongue and thought about taking a snort, but, like the food inside the restaurant, he decided against it. He remembered that the reason he was already late was the cute little brown-haired truckstop mamma from last night and the fantastic white powder that had brought them together and kept them that way most of the night. Although she was just a memory now, another one-night stand, at least the coke was still in the sleeper with him and one out of two wasn't bad.

Cummings worked his way out of the sleeper into the driver's seat. The Freightliner idled like a sleeping kitten's purr. Cummings looked at the fuel gauge . . . half-full. There was a vacuum bottle that should be full of coffee somewhere in the cab. Cummings looked for it under the clothes that cluttered the passenger's seat. He found it underneath his wrinkled jeans, but somehow during the night's activities it had slipped open and spilled. Cummings turned it botom-side up and drained the last quarter-cup of cold coffee into the lid cup. Then he found his shirt, wrinkled like his pants, and rummaged through the breast pocket. They were there—pickle park specials: amphetamines.

His fingers were still asleep and lacked the agility needed to unwrap the aluminum foil that kept them secure. Finally, they were free. Cummings popped both hits of speed into his mouth and washed them down with the last remnants of the cold coffee.

It took ten minutes for him to get his clothes and boots back on. When that was finished, he flexed his fingers in an attempt to stimulate the circulation. They were tingling and felt slightly numb. He wrote it off to sleeping like a dead man in all the wrong positions. His bulging biceps hurt and he had an occasional pain in the lower back. Despite the sleep (what little there had been), Cummings still didn't feel rested. When he looked into the mirror to comb his thinning brown hair, he realized he looked just about as bad as he felt—like somebody had beaten him and left him for dead. But then that's what he paid the mammas for, to wear him completely out. He felt a certain sense of deep satisfaction knowing that the old gal who climbed into the sleeper last night had earned her money. And from what he could remember, she had been worth every dime of the forty bucks.

Cummings ran his tingling fingers through his thick brown beard. "Okay, Larry baby, get your shit together and let's get to truckin'."

He released the parking brake and dropped the Freightliner into gear. The clutch came out unsteadily and the big rig lept forward with a jerk. He dropped the clutch back to the floor and tapped on the accelerator in short, rapid strokes. The diesel engine perked back to life and he let the clutch out once again, this time steadily and slowly.

The rig crept across the truckstop parking lot until it reached the main roadway. Cummings looked both ways before he pulled onto the highway. That's when he realized his vision was blurred. Maybe it was from too much coke or not enough real rest, but whatever it was, he wasn't going to let it stop the delivery. He had, after all, driven with worse crud in his eyes when he had a summer head cold. No big deal.

The Freightliner was halfway into a left turn when Cummings heard the blaring car horn and screaming tires from behind him. He glanced into the rearview Westcoast mirrors and saw a four-wheeler skidding sideways toward him. He reached up and yanked on the cord to sound the airhorn. It blared a loud warning and then Cummings pressed harder on the accelerator. Once the rig was straightened out on the highway, he rolled the driver's window down, crammed his arm out, and shot the four-wheeler a finger. As he turned onto the entry ramp to Interstate 75, he mumbled something about how stupid four-wheeler drivers were.

At last, the rig was rolling south on the superslap. If Lady Luck would park her sweet, tender loins on his dashboard, he could make up for lost time. If she didn't, then it was drivers-beware, because Larry Cummings was hell-bound and determined to make the delivery on time. Seventy-eight thousand pounds of rolling thunder was going to cut a swatch across Ohio and back up to the docks right on schedule.

The big eighteen-wheeler rolled like a snowball headed downhill for ten minutes. Nothing slowed it, nothing stopped it. But then the four-wheeler, driven by a pair of legs in a white miniskirt, cut sharply in front of the rig and stomped on the brakes for the next exit. Cummings stepped on the airbrakes and black smoke rolled from beneath the big rig. Burning rubber smeared into the pavement as the rig rocked and groaned.

The driver of the compact four-wheeler was oblivious to the fact that nearly forty tons of steel machinery was coming at her with the same lethal potential of a steamroller flattening an ant.

Cummings cursed loudly. "You crazy bitch!" He jerked hard to the left and narrowly missed the rear of the little compact car. The rig resisted the sudden turn by screaming and moaning with the sound of metal stressed to the threshhold of disaster. At last, Cummings regained control. He shook his head, trying to clear his vision. He looked ahead and scanned the traffic through cloudy eyes. He took a deep breath and let it out. "Shit, man, damned four-wheelers. I sure could use a drink."

Cummings settled into the seat after he turned the audio level up on the console CB radio. He listened to the northbound eighteen-wheelers telling other southbound rigs about a major traffic tie-up twenty miles ahead in a construction zone. Although his fingers were still a little numb, he managed to draw a cigarette from his shirt pocket and get it lit. He took a soothing draw to calm his nerves. When he glanced at the speedometer, it was showing seventy-eight miles per hour. "All right, you highway menaces, I'm hammer down and comin' through town. Step on the gas or I'll run over your ass." Then he laughed so hard his head hurt.

———

"Come on, kids, get inside. Please stop fooling around. If you want to meet Daddy for lunch, we've got to hurry." Julie Foster shuffled her two children into the van like a mother hen rounding up baby chicks.

Errin spoke first. "Mommie, where are we gonna meet Daddy?"

Before Julie could answer, Eric interrupted. "I want to go to McDonald's. Please, Mommie, can we go to McDonald's to eat?"

Julie warded off the inherent parental frustration and forced a smile. "Now, listen, let's all cooperate. We went to McDonald's last time, Eric. Today, Daddy wants us to meet him at the Captain's Fish Dock. We can't always live on hamburgers, you know."

Errin yelled. "Yeah! I love the Captain's fish and chips. Oh boy, fries with lots of ketchup."

"Mommie, can I have shrimp? I love shrimp. And maybe some of that red sauce stuff." Eric was jumping on the back seat and making no effort to conceal his happiness.

"Wait until we get there, Eric. You might change your mind."

"Oh, no I won't. I like that red sauce and those pieces of lemon."

Errin made a silly face. "Mommie, don't let Eric eat those lemon slices in front of me. It makes my mouth feel funny when he does that. Yuk!"

Julie steered the van from the driveway and onto the quiet suburban street. "Errin, let him eat what he wants. If it bothers you, don't look at him."

Errin shot back, "Really, Mommie, it's yuk. How can he eat that stuff? I bet if I had a sister, she wouldn't eat lemon."

"Shut up, Errin. I'll eat it that way if I want to. Mommie just said I could. Didn't you, Mommie?"

Julie stopped the van at the end of the street at a stop sign. She looked carefully both ways and made a left turn. "Yes, Eric, I did. Now, both of you, calm down. Let's not be arguing when we pick up Daddy at the office. All right?"

Both kids nodded.

"Good. Now I want both of you to—"

Eric interrupted. "Are you sure we have to go to the fish place, Mommie? Can't we go to McDonald's?"

"No McDonald's today, Eric. It's definitely fish. I thought you liked the red sauce."

"Oh, I do, but I like the toys in the Happy Meals, too. I was just checking to see if you'd changed your mind."

Julie almost laughed out loud. "No, Eric, I haven't changed my mind." She signaled her intention to turn onto the entry ramp to Interstate 75. She made the turn and accelerated out the ramp until she was in the flow of traffic. No sooner had she rounded the first curve on the four-lane highway than she had to decelerate. Ahead, the four lanes were reduced to two by massive construction.

Orange- and white-striped plastic barrels lined the highway and brought the lanes into a merger of two slow-moving southbound lanes. And in front of her, cars coasted to a stop and blocked the highway.

Eric sensed the change and looked out the front windshield. "What's wrong, Mommie? Why are we stopping?"

"Traffic, darling. It's backed up. Maybe I should have taken Carpenter Street instead of the outer loop."

Errin had to get a word in to ensure that Eric didn't have the opportunity to talk more than she did. "Are we going to be late for Daddy's lunch, Mommie?"

"No, Errin. It's still moving a little. We have enough time to get there. We can't be late for Daddy's lunch. This is a special occasion. He doesn't get the chance to do this every day. This is special."

Julie Foster glanced into the rearview mirror out of habit and saw forty tons of rolling death coming at her. In a double take, she thought her eyes were deceiving her. Then, in a heartbeat, a weak, sickening feeling of helplessness rushed through her body. She knew there was no way the speeding tractor-trailer could stop. It was traveling much too fast. Then she saw the vehicle skidding, then sliding. The big truck was out of control and there was no way out. She knew it was going to crash into the van and she had to do something to save the children. Out of instinct, she screamed. "Oh, my God! Children, get down on the floor. He's going to hit us. Oh, God! Oh, no! David, I love you." The last thing Julie Foster heard before everything went dark and silent was the sound of metal tearing through metal and the children screaming. Then the van shook with a thunderous roar and it muffled the children's screams and the fire was everywhere.

———

David Foster watched and listened. The veins in his temples protruded, but his face remained a work of stone. Expressionless. The words spoken by the minister were meaningless and they flashed through his mind like fleeting strokes of lightning on some distant horizon. And the faces of relatives and friends . . . he scanned them, taking inventory one by one. He saw them, but he didn't really *see* them because nothing registered with his mind. Tears, sobs, and sadness etched every face standing at the graveside . . . every face except his own. And now, three days into his new lonely world, there were no more tears and no more emotions to be spilled from the fractured crevices of his heart.

The minister stopped talking, folded his Bible against his chest, and stepped away from the three coffins that would soon be lowered into the earth. David Foster stepped forward. He placed a single red rose on the first coffin, knelt, and gently kissed the vessel that would harbor a member of his family forever. He stood and repeated the process two more times. When he stood from the last coffin, he stepped away and stood beside a row of chairs that had been occupied by his remaining closest relatives and his wife's relatives.

The minister spoke with a saddened heart. "And so, dear God, we return these blessed innocent souls into your coveted arms. And we ask that you keep them safely in your covenant until the time you choose to reunite this lovely family. And, dear God, show those among the family and friends of these beloved deceased a way to understand and accept this horrible tragedy. And let the dust of these earthly bodies return to the dust of the earth from which they came. And take the innocent souls, dear God, to your Heavenly home. Amen."

Slowly, the coffins descended silently into the cold ground. The people gathered at the graveside moved away in a procession of black-clad mourners. David Foster watched, the scene etched in his mind forever. His family, his life, everything he had ever known and loved, descended into the ground before his eyes. And when the last coffin was laid to rest, he turned away.

ABOUT THE AUTHOR

Bob Ham was raised in the Blue Ridge Mountains, just outside Roanoke, Virginia. He attended college in Roanoke and later studied law.

Bob has an extensive background in law enforcement, with experience ranging from traffic patrol to highly detailed undercover operations involving narcotics and firearms.

In the mid-seventies, he relocated to Nashville, Tennessee, where he gave up law enforcement for a successful career in the country music business. Bob now owns a record promotion and marketing firm that has continuously set industry track records since its inception in 1980.

In addition to his music and law enforcement interests, Bob Ham is also an authority on radio communications and firearms. As for the latter, he is currently a qualified Expert with both shotgun and submachine gun, and a qualified Master with the pistol and revolver. He occasionally competes in regional law enforcement competitions as a member of the Williamson County Sheriff's Department combat pistol team.

Licensed as an Advanced Class amateur radio operator, Bob is active on the amateur radio bands and has made thousands of radio contacts throughout the world. This hobby also affords him the opportunity to experiment with various types of antennas and electronic devices, including computers, packet radio, and radioteletype. This extensive hands-on knowledge in fire arms, law enforcement, electronics, and radio blends together to make Bob Ham's OVERLOAD series both entertaining and factual.

He currently resides in Brentwood, Tennessee, with his wife and children.

Action on Eighteen Wheels!

Marc Lee and Carl Browne, ex-Delta Force anti-terrorist commandos: They've taken on bloodthirsty Middle Eastern terrorists...deadly drug cartels...vicious bikers...the Mafia...no matter how badly they're outnumbered, Lee and Browne always come up swinging...and blasting!

Don't miss any of the exciting books in Bob Ham's OVERLOAD SERIES!

Now there are two great ways to catch up with your favorite thrillers